SILVER

SILVER

NORMA FOX MAZER

MORROW JUNIOR BOOKS/NEW YORK

YA

Printed in the United States of America.
1 2 3 4 5 6 7 8 9 10

Library of Congress Cataloging-in-Publication Data
Mazer, Norma Fox, 1931–
Silver / by Norma Fox Mazer.
p.   cm.
Summary: Despite their different backgrounds, Sarabeth, a teenager
living with her mother in a trailer and transferring to a new
school, makes friends with Grant and her affluent friends, including
troubled Patty who shares a painful secret about her uncle.
ISBN 0-688-06865-0
[1. Friendship—Fiction. 2. Child molesting—Fiction.]
I. Title.
PZ7.M47398Si 1988
[Fic]—dc 19   88-18652   CIP
                    AC

FOR MY FRIENDS
Elisabeth Ellingson and Nancy Woodson

SILVER

CHAPTER

Mom says I'm not to worry about money. "It's my business, Sarabeth," she tells me at least once a day. I don't *worry* about money, but I admit I do think about it quite a bit.

Mom has a bunch of little envelopes that say things like RENT, FOOD, GAS, CAR REPAIRS, DENTIST that she keeps in a shoe box. Every day when she comes home from work, she takes the money she earned from cleaning houses and divides it up. She tries to put something in every envelope. If there's any money left over, she puts it in the envelope that says WE NEED.

"What do you need?" Leo said one day, watching Mom put five dollars in that envelope.

Mom gave him a look. "Everything," she said.

It does seem that way. If it isn't gym shorts for me or Mom's special toothpaste, then it's stamps or shampoo or sneakers or any of a hundred other things. Mom should have a watch, the back left burner on the stove doesn't work, the faucet in the bathroom makes a hideous noise when you turn it on, and practically all my underwear is torn.

I like the WE NEED envelope. I like seeing it fill up with dollar bills. Mom's rule is that we save twenty dollars before we buy anything. Then we decide what we need most. The stove doesn't absolutely have to be fixed, but I really need new underpants. Last year, I was exactly Mom's height, and we wore each other's jeans and shirts. That helped a lot. Then I started springing up, passing her, growing out of everything. Now it seems as if every time we get twenty dollars, we spend it on me.

We also have a coin jar we keep on the counter in the kitchen, one of those big round pickle jars. One time, a man Mom worked for paid her with a tin can full of pennies. Mom dumped the pennies on the table and asked me to count them. "Should be fifteen dollars exactly in there, hon."

I made piles of pennies on the table, twenty pennies to a pile. "Eleven dollars and eighty-six cents, Mom."

"Count it again, Sarabeth."

I started over. Mom was soaking her feet in a

pan of hot water. "Eleven dollars and eighty-*seven* cents," I said.

"Do it again. He's a lawyer; I can't believe he'd stiff me like that!"

I counted the pennies two more times. Same result.

"Oooh!" Mom made a terrible face. She went to the phone and called Mr. Kingsley to tell him he'd made a mistake and shortchanged her. She explained how I counted the pennies four times.

He didn't believe her.

"I don't lie," she said to him. "Do you think I would lie for a miserable three dollars and thirteen cents?" When she hung up, she was almost crying. She hardly ever cries. She says she did all her crying when my father died. "I'll never work for that man again. I'm going to throw his stinking pennies into the garbage!"

"No, Mom, we can use them."

"I know! Oooh. *Ooooh!* That makes me so mad." The pennies went into the pickle jar.

The winter I was ten years old, even the pickle jar was empty. Mom had the flu and couldn't work for a long time. We had no money coming in, and we had to ask for welfare.

The county sent a social worker to see us. He wore a blue parka with a fur-lined hood. He stamped his feet and looked everywhere around our house. "Cold in this place," he said. He shoved his hands in his pockets. "You like living in a trailer?" He asked Mom a lot of questions. Mom answered his questions in her *lady* voice, her telephone voice, her "Yes, I'll be glad to clean your house" voice. A voice I hated.

After the social worker left, Mom and I got into a fight. It seemed to be about spaghetti. We'd had spaghetti for supper every night that week, and we were having it again. "I'm not eating that," I said.

"And I'm not throwing good food into the garbage, Sarabeth." Mom pushed me to the table.

"Where's your sweet *lady* voice now?" I yelled.

"Sit down! You're staying there until you clean your plate." She put the spaghetti in front of me.

I didn't eat it. I sat there for so long I fell asleep.

I woke up in the middle of the night. Everything was dark and quiet. Mom was across from me, sleeping with her head on the table. My cat, Tobias, was curled up on top of the refrigerator.

In the morning, the sun came in through the window over the sink. I woke up to see Mom watching me. She pushed the hair out of her face. "Stubborn," she said, touching the plate of cold spaghetti with one finger.

I sat up. "Don't try to give it to me for breakfast. I'm not eating it."

"Oh, now, be quiet," she said. She pulled me onto her lap and wrapped her arms around me. Then she kissed me and pointed to her cheek, and I kissed her. That was how we made up.

Mom warmed the spaghetti for herself for breakfast. She made me cinnamon and sugar toast and hot whipped powdered milk with coffee. It tasted so good!

I was in my old school then, Morrisview Central. I'd never gone to any other school and never thought I would, until a couple of years later when Mom happened to see a map of the trailer park in Fred and Dolly Krall's office. She took me over there to show me what she'd discovered. "Look at this, Sarabeth," she said, poking her finger at the map. "Look at it carefully, because this is going to make a big difference to you."

On the map, Roadview Trailer Park looked like a witch's hat. Most of the hat was in the Morrisview school district, but the peak of the hat—the part of the trailer park that was up against the cliff—was in the Drumlins school district. "The best schools in the county," Mom said. "That's where we want you to go, hon." On the way back to our trailer, she said, "Did you notice that only One, Two, and Three are in the Drumlins school district?"

I'd noticed. Fred and Dolly, who owned Roadview, lived in One. Old Mr. Rafer lived in Two, and the Floreys lived in Three. I'd lived here all my life, and I knew everyone. At that time, we lived in Sixteen.

"One of these days," Mom said, "someone is going to move out."

"Who, Mom? Not Fred and Dolly."

"Someone," Mom said stubbornly. "And when they do, we move in."

I thought Mom was wrong, and I was glad. I liked Sixteen. It was my home. I loved it. I had friends at school, but they didn't come home with me. I didn't ask them. I was a homebody, a home person. I never minded being home alone. My best times, my favorite times, though, were when Mom was home, too. We'd lie around, eating popcorn and talking. And all the better if it was raining, the windows wet and smeary, the rain tapping on the trailer roof. Chilly and wet outside, but inside warm and cozy.

One night Mom and I were in her room. Mom was lying on the bed, propped up against the pillows, reading the newspaper. I was sitting crosslegged near her, studying. I wished for popcorn, but one of our rules is no eating in Mom's room. Tobias, for once, was being good. He had his head on my knee and he was purring. This cat of mine is all white, with one little orange splash over his left eye.

He likes to fool around. He'll grab my skin between his teeth—he won't break it, though—and he'll hold on and growl, giving me a fake bite, his way of saying, "Come on, Sarabeth, let's play!"

"Look at this," Mom said. She sat up. "It says right here that Drumlins school district has the best teachers and the most opportunities for kids." She held the newspaper out to me. "Read it for yourself. You see, hon, those kids always score the highest on the state tests, and they walk off with all the scholarships and prizes, too."

"Maybe they're just smart, Mom."

"No smarter than you. Never say that! That district does more for its kids because it has more money." Mom pushed her hair behind her ears. "Those folks with the big houses and the big cars and the big paychecks pay big school taxes. You think those schools operate with envelopes like us? If they did, it would be a million in this one, a half million in that one. They have swimming pools and tennis courts in those schools. They have the best stuff in their science labs. They have everything. If we have a chance to get you in there, we're taking it. People like us have to—"

"What do you mean, people like *us?*"

"I mean people like *us,* Sarabeth. People who live in trailer parks. We have to look out for opportunities. We have to use everything we can."

"Okay, Mom, okay." It would never happen. Why would Mr. Rafer move? Why would the Floreys? Why would anyone?

"You never know," Mom said.

She was right. In May, old Mr. Rafer broke his hip. When he got out of the hospital, he went to live with his daughter in Michigan. A week later, Leo and Cynthia helped us move. Out of my dear old Sixteen, where I'd always lived, into Two. Out of my old school district and into DSD.

CHAPTER 2

New bus, new school, new class, new kids.

Besides that, Mom had the flu and hadn't worked all week. That always upset me. That first morning I was tense. I found my homeroom without any trouble, but then I stood near the door, looking in. Go in, I told myself. Kids pushed past me, talking and laughing. It looked as if they all knew each other.

I remembered what Mom had said before I left. "You go in there and act like you've always been there, hon." She was in bed with a hot washcloth wrapped around her throat. "Don't let anyone put you down," she croaked.

I walked in and sat down. No one talked to me. I glanced around. Everyone looked snobby and rich.

I tried not to think about my old school.

The teacher rapped on the desk. "Good morning, everyone. I'm Mr. Light." He was wearing a flannel shirt with a loose tie. "Let's get to know each other. I'm new here."

"We're not," a boy said from the back of the room.

"I gather that," Mr. Light said. "Do you people all know each other? You have an advantage over me. Not for long, though." He opened his roll book. "Richard Adamski? There you are. Big guy, aren't you?"

"I guess so," Richard Adamski said.

"June Allen. Where are you? Doing a crossword puzzle? Good mental activity." Mr. Light went around the room, saying something to everyone. "Do you like to read? . . . What's your favorite sport? . . . How many hours a day do you watch TV?" To one girl, Jean Lowdan, he said, "You look like a serious student, Jean."

The closer he got to me, the tenser I felt. What was he going to ask me? *Where do you live? Why are you in this school? Don't you belong in Morrisview?*

"Sarabeth Silver?"

I put up my hand.

"Transfer from the Morrisview school district. Are you going to like it here?" I shrugged. "Quiet one, eh? How do you like it so far?"

"Okay, I guess."

A blonde girl I'd noticed before turned to look at me. She was wearing a green jump suit. Her hair was pulled up at each side with green combs. She frowned. Maybe I should have been more tactful or sounded more enthusiastic.

Mr. Light kept going around the room. "Nissa Tucker . . . Mike Umberto . . . Grant Varrow . . ." Grant was the girl who'd frowned. "Grant!" Mr. Light said. "Where'd you get that name?"

"It's my mother's family name."

I liked the quiet, dignified way she answered. There was something special about her, something not ordinary. Most people slumped or slouched or stuck their feet out in the aisle. Grant Varrow sat in the center of her seat, her back perfectly straight. She seemed serene, calm.

I started imagining being her friend, riding the bus with her after school. We'd sit together and talk. We'd go to my home, and we'd talk some more and play with Tobias. It was strange for me to be thinking that. Me, who never brought anyone home.

In the last few minutes, Mr. Light passed out schedules and cards. "Fill the cards out. You all know your phone numbers and the name of the person to be notified if . . . et cetera, et cetera. Leave the cards on my desk as you go."

The bell rang, and everyone crowded toward the

door and into the hall. I walked behind Grant. I only had to take a single step to be next to her. A skinny girl with curly red hair darted by, bumping into me. "Oops, sorry," I said. She didn't say a word. Her eyes slid right over me. She caught up to Grant and threw her arm around her. They walked up the hall together, then the red-haired girl turned off into a classroom.

I kept walking behind Grant. I had to go upstairs to Room 35. I decided that if Grant went upstairs, too, I would catch up to her and speak to her. I followed her to the staircase. She went down, and I went up.

CHAPTER 3

Tobias was curled up on the blue rug near Mom's bed when I came home. They were both sleeping. I made a sandwich and took it outside to eat on the steps. Mrs. Prang, who lived in Four, was raking her yard. She waved to me. The Prangs were new people; they'd only lived in Roadview five or six months. They came here from Cambodia.

Roadview Trailer Park is set between a cliff and Highway I-81. In good weather some people put their chairs out facing the road. Then if there's an accident, they get to see it first and report it to everyone else. But when I want to look at something, I don't choose the road. I choose the cliff.

I don't know why I like looking at the cliff so much. It's very high—at least a hundred feet—and it's rocky and sheer, with only a few scrawny ever-greens growing slantwise out of it. After a hard rain, rocks and dirt slide down, and Mom always worries about a landslide. Last summer, the city sent engineers to check things out. Three of them tramped around in boots for a day, making measurements.

"If they say it's unsafe, we'll have to move," Mom said. "Then where will we go?"

"Oh, Mom, they won't say that."

"You never know," she said, and I shut up. The last time she'd said *You never know,* she'd been right.

I used to play near the cliff when I was small. One of my games was pretending it was a magic mountain, and my father was coming up on the other side. I'd stare at the top for hours, the sun in my eyes, waiting for him to appear.

In our old trailer, I couldn't see the cliff from my bedroom window. I saw Fourteen, where the Lawsons kept their dog tied up day and night. Poor Heidi was always whining and howling. I wasn't the only one who minded. Tobias refused to come into my room, or if he did he sat on the sill and hissed.

When I went inside again, Tobias and Mom were both awake. I gave Tobias some cat chewies and fixed a tray for Mom. I poured orange juice into a blue glass, cut toast in triangles, and made a cheese omelet. Cooking is a specialty of mine, and someday I'd like to go to cooking school. If I become a famous chef, I plan to write a cookbook, *Sarabeth's Sublime and Superb Recipes for Every Occasion.* I already have some original recipes, like my Broiled Open-Faced Peanut-Butter/Banana Sandwich. What I do is mash peanut butter and banana together, add cinnamon and nutmeg, spread it on bread, broil it, and then—this is the really original part—sprinkle on grated Parmesan cheese.

I carried the tray into Mom's room, which I call "the clean blue scene." Her quilt is light blue, she has a dark-blue velvet pillow, there are blue venetian blinds on the windows, and everything is superneat. Mom's floor never has junk on it, her bed is always smooth and unwrinkled (except when she's in it, of course, or when I am), and all the things in her bureau drawers are in neat piles. I'm not like that at all.

Mom held out her cheek for a kiss. "I didn't hear you come home."

"You were sleeping. Did you sleep all day?"

"Mostly. Got up once for the phone. No, twice. Cynthia. Then Leo." Leo is Mom's boyfriend. He's younger than she is, which bothers Mom, but not Leo.

While she ate, I sat on the bed and told Mom about school. "My homeroom teacher talks a lot. I don't know how I feel about him. I like the language-arts teacher, Mr.—oh, I forget his name. And—lemme see—what else?"

"Don't say 'lemme,' hon." She nibbled the toast. "It sounds ignorant. *Let. Me.*"

"Yeah, okay."

"*Yes.* Okay."

"Mom! You want to hear any more or not?"

"Did you meet anybody you like?" Mom harps on my having more friends. When she was my age, she had five girlfriends who were always in each other's houses. "Who'd you eat lunch with?" she asked.

"Mom, it's only the first day." I thought of Grant Varrow. I'd seen her eating with the redhead and two other girls.

"Did you get lost?"

"Why? Where? The bus took me right to school."

Mom blew her nose. "I mean in school. My first day in junior high school, I got lost six times."

"Wow, that's pretty"—I was going to say "dumb," but I stopped myself and said—"pretty bad." Mom is sensitive about words like *dumb* and *stupid* because she didn't graduate from high school.

"Were you scared?" she asked.

"Not really."

"Good for you, hon. My first day in junior high, I was scared. Really was. I was a very shy kid."

It's hard for me to imagine Mom scared or shy. I wonder if she was that way when she married my father. She was sixteen and pregnant with me. My father was seventeen. You might think they had to get married—well, they did—but they were in love and they were going to get married anyway. "It was no shotgun wedding," my mother always says. "Once you were on the way, we wanted you, hon. You just decided to show up in our lives a little sooner than we'd planned on."

Some nights I lie in bed and try to remember my father, try to remember something about him— anything, really. His name was Benjamin Robert Silver. I think that's a beautiful name. If he were alive, I know he would be a great dad. In every picture in our album he's got this grin, like he's looking out at the world and laughing about things. And Mom says that's the way he was, good-natured and loving.

I don't think I'm that good-natured, but according to Mom, even though I look more like her, I'm more like my father in character. One thing of his in looks that I do have are my thumbs. They're weird thumbs, flat and broad. I don't know anyone else who has thumbs like that. I wish I liked them, since they come to me from my father, but I'm self-conscious about them. I'm always tucking them into my palms.

Mom's family blamed my father for Mom's getting pregnant and having to leave school. My father's family blamed Mom for his getting married too young and having to go to work. Everybody was mad at everybody else. Nobody, except Mom and Dad, wanted me to be born. They lived in southern Pennsylvania then, but they moved away from their families to central New York State.

My father got a job on a construction crew, building houses near the Rome air base. Mom says that even though things weren't easy, it was a great time for them. "We had three and a half years. Beautiful years."

Then one day, driving home from work in his pickup truck, my father was killed in an accident on the interstate. "I went a little bit crazy then," Mom told me. "I couldn't believe he was gone. You know how much I loved your daddy? I can't even tell you. There are no words for me to say what I felt about that sweet boy."

"*Boy,* Mom?"

"He wasn't even twenty-one when he died, hon. I'd loved him for almost half my life, ever since I laid eyes on him when I was in eighth grade. If it wasn't for you, I don't think I would have gone on living. I would have just laid myself down on my bed and waited for everything to end."

The accident was a freak. Two tandem wheels flew off a truck hauling paving stones. One of the wheels hit my father's pickup truck and crushed the roof like a piece of paper. He died instantly.

For a while the police thought the truck driver was drunk, but he was under the legal limit of alcohol. He was charged with driving an uninspected motor vehicle and carrying more weight than the legal limit. He had to pay a two-hundred-dollar fine. Mom got a settlement from the insurance company. It paid for my father's funeral and kept us going for six months. Then we were on our own.

CHAPTER 4

Almost every morning that week, I was in homeroom early. I'd take out my notebook and check my schedule or go over math problems, but all the time I was really watching the door, waiting for Grant Varrow to appear. She was always with someone else, the redhead or another blonde girl or a dark, plump girl she called Asa. They'd stand in the doorway, talking. Asa had a laugh you could hear all across the room, but Grant's laugh was like everything else about her—beautiful, quiet, serene. I imagined that if I was with her, I'd lean in close so I could hear every word she said.

Sometimes I'd catch a bit of their conversation. Asa was always talking about books. Grant teased her. "How many books did you read last night?"

Once I heard Grant saying, ". . . and he said my embouchure is improving." I wrote it in my notebook: *Grant says someone says her armbrashure (spelling? meaning????) is improving.* I wrote down other things I heard her say and things I noticed about her—that she carried a flute case, had two silver rings on her thumb, wore a necklace of green glass beads.

In homeroom, my seat was two rows over and three seats ahead of Grant's. Sometimes, waiting for the first bell to ring, I'd sharpen a pencil and pass her desk. I didn't speak to her. In a way, I didn't dare. She seemed so wonderful, so far above me. From the way she dressed and talked, I knew she was rich, but it was more than that: she had friends, she was always with those other three girls. What possible interest could she have in me?

If I saw Grant coming toward me in the hall, I'd start checking my books, acting like I was so busy thinking about important things I didn't even notice her. Later I'd be mad at myself, I'd think how stupidly I'd acted. Then the next time I saw her, I'd quickly say, "Hi!" She always answered in a friendly but remote way, so I could never be sure if she even knew who I was.

At lunch in the cafeteria, she ate with her friends. I sat down where I could watch them. I noticed how they all turned to Grant and listened when she talked. When they got up to leave, they clustered around her.

By the end of the week, I knew who the other three girls were. Asa Goronkian was the plump, dark one with the big laugh. The redhead was Jennifer Rosen, skinny, freckled, with a tiny face and wild, frizzy hair. Patty Lewis was the beauty. She had long blonde hair, very red cheeks, and full red lips.

Sometimes I'd say the names of Grant's friends to myself, recite them softly under my breath. "Jennifer Rosen. Patty Lewis. Asa Goronkian." Then I'd add my name, "Sarabeth Silver."

Asa and I were in language arts together. She was funny and smart, probably the biggest brain in the class. I had no classes with Patty—I only saw her in the halls or the cafeteria—but I had gym with Jennifer three times a week. She was skinny, but strong and athletic. She was the only girl in the class who could do the pegboard, and when Mr. Cooper wanted someone to demonstrate that or rope climbing, he called on her. "Come on, Freckles, show 'em how it's done."

One day we had a fire drill in the middle of gym, and leaving the building, Jennifer and I ended up in line together. "You're new here," she said.

I nodded. "I'm Sarabeth Silver."

"Hi." She twisted her hand through her hair.

"You're Jennifer Rosen." She didn't seem surprised that I knew her name. She asked me where I lived. "Roadview Trailer Park," I said, "near Southwood Corners."

"You live in a trailer?"

"Yes."

"You really do?" She looked horrified. "What's it like?"

"It's fine."

"What do you do when you have to go?"

What did she mean? "Excuse me?" I said.

"I mean, especially in winter, what do you do when you have to go?" she repeated.

I stared at her. Did she think we had an outhouse? "I do the same thing you do," I said after a moment. "Open the door, go into the bathroom, close the door, pick up the toilet lid—"

"You have a regular bathroom in your trailer? Oh, good!" she said, as if I'd won first prize in a tough contest. "But, still, winter . . . Isn't it cold without heat?"

"You bet. But we keep little ice picks by our beds, so when we wake up in the morning, we can crack the ice on our bodies."

Then it was her turn to stare at me. When she got it, she gave me a stiff little smile.

"How was school today?" Mom said at supper that night.

"Okay."

"Why so quiet?"

"No reason." I was thinking about Jennifer and Grant, thinking that even if by some miracle I became friends with Grant, I'd never make it with Jennifer. Not that I wanted to! I didn't like her little peaky, snobby face, I didn't like her wiry red hair, and I especially didn't like the things she said. *What do you do when you have to go?*

"Things are going all right?" Mom said.

"Sure."

"Any problems?"

"Not really." Then I said, "It's a snobby school, Mom."

"Oh, come on, Sarabeth, everybody in the school can't be a snob."

"Oh, no?"

"Listen, hon, even where I went to school, in my little town, there were snobs and snoots. So what? Ignore them!"

I could easily ignore Jennifer for the next two hundred years, but the way I felt about Grant, even if she was the snobbiest person in the world, she could ignore *me* for the next two *thousand* years and I'd still like her.

"If someone has flies up her nose, that's her problem," Mom went on. "Don't waste your valuable self on people like that."

"Mom, it's okay for you to talk, you don't have

to go to school, you don't know what it's like. You're grown-up and free and independent."

"Oh, boy!" She put her chin in her hands. "If you knew what you just said. Wait till I tell Cynthia!"

"Mom! Don't tell Cynthia everything I say. I'm not a little kid anymore."

"Grown-up and free and independent," she repeated. She couldn't stop laughing. "Well, grown-up, anyway, hon, you got that part right."

In a way, I wanted to take Mom's advice. I knew it would be better for me if I could ignore Grant. It was embarrassing how much I liked her. I watched her all the time. I thought about her too much. Was I going to see her next period? Should I say something? Or nothing? Smile, or just nod? How should I act? Interested? Lively? Casual? Maybe I could borrow something from her, a piece of paper or a pen. Then she would *have* to talk to me. No, scratch that. I didn't want her to think I was the sort of person who was always borrowing stuff and hanging around.

Once I came up behind Grant as she was taking a drink at the water fountain near the office. I had a strong impulse to go up to her and say, "Did you have a good drink? Was the water cold? Are you still thirsty?" I had to control myself to keep from doing it.

For a while I wondered if I should take flute lessons. Grant played the flute in the school orchestra. We'd have something in common. Maybe I should just start a conversation about music. Stop her in the hall and tell her I'd always wanted to learn guitar.

Great. She'd think I was a lunatic.

I kept thinking of ways to become friends with Grant and then discarding them.

Follow Grant home, sleep on her steps, and jump up in the morning pleading, "I need to be your friend!"

Write Grant an anonymous letter, telling her she was missing a tremendous chance for a special friendship with Sarabeth Silver.

Phone her, disguise my voice, and say, "Grant Varrow? This is a tip from someone with your best interests at heart. Sarabeth Silver would be a better friend to you than anyone you know."

Plan after plan went down the drain. All my ideas had one thing in common—they were dumb, desperate, and totally unworkable.

There was more. *Grant flunks out in math and Sarabeth tutors her, thereby earning Grant's eternal gratitude and friendship.*

Grant falls and breaks a bone. Fortunately for her, Sarabeth Silver is on the scene and knows exactly what to do. Were it not for Sarabeth Silver, Grant Varrow would have lost her leg. She throws her arms around Sarabeth Silver and vows lifelong devotion.

Grant is sick and needs a transfusion of a rare blood type. Guess who's the only person for thousands of miles around with the same rare blood type? After the transfusion, Grant holds Sarabeth's hand and says, with tears in her eyes, "I will never forget. We are blood sisters forever."

Naturally, in my sane moments, I knew all these thoughts were absurd. My blood was type O, like everyone else's. I didn't want Grant to flunk math, break her bones, or be deathly ill. All I wanted was for her to see me and like me, the way I liked her.

One day, as I was going into the girls' room, I passed Grant coming out. She was wearing a long green dress and amber earrings. She glanced at me and her eyebrows went up. She was blonde, but she had dark, thick eyebrows. Her eyebrows went up. What did that mean? Was she sending me a message?

Grant to Sarabeth, hello.

Or was the message *Hello, aren't you what's-her-face . . . ?*

Or maybe it was *Good grief, why am I always running into you?*

After thinking about this for the next hour, I became convinced that Grant *had* meant to speak to me, but I'd rushed by her too fast. Much as I wanted her to speak to me, *ached* for that, I never, never slowed down when I saw her.

CHAPTER 5

"Let me look at you," Cynthia said. She hugged me. "I haven't seen you all week!"

"I've been in school," I said.

She sniffed. "What're you baking?"

"Cookies. I was going to bring you over some later."

"Chocolate chip?" she asked hopefully.

"Mint chip. Save some for Billy, he always likes my mint chip cookies. . . . Why are you dressed up?" Cynthia was an entertainer. She called herself a café singer, but lots of her jobs turned out to be in regular smelly bars that just had fancy names, like "Le Parisienne" or "Café de Brazil." "Are you going to work?" I asked. She was wearing a black dress with gold pinstripes and huge padded shoulders.

She shook her head. "Just showing off. New dress. Like it?"

"Sort of big shoulders."

"That's the *idea,* toots!"

"Just *asking,* toots!" Cynthia was Mom's best friend and sort of a second mother to me. She and Billy lived in Twenty-Two.

Mom said Cynthia saved her sanity after my father died. "She hung in there with me. She came over every day to see me, she let me cry and scream and say crazy, mean, horrible things about the world."

Before Cynthia's career as a singer got going, I used to stay with her a lot when I was little and Mom went out to work. I would also go along with Mom plenty of times to her jobs—in fact, that was why she got into cleaning houses. She figured it was the kind of work where she could bring me along. Still, I was with Cynthia enough to think she was part of my family. I even called her Ma Cynthia for a while.

Once, in second grade, the teacher asked us to draw our family as animals. The first thing I did was draw a bright yellow sun. Then I drew my father like a happy water bug, shiny brown and floating on his back in a blue heaven. I put in our trailer, and, outside it, Mom as a mouse, because she's so small, and me as a cat, because I purred when Mom rubbed my back. Finally, I drew Cynthia as a beautiful long-faced horse, shaking her black mane.

"Do I hear Cynthia?" Mom said, coming into the kitchen. They kissed each other. Mom noticed Cynthia's dress right away, too. "Whew, what shoulders! The Green Bay Packers are going to recruit you, gal."

"These shoulders are supposed to make me look so powerful everybody will shut up and listen when I'm singing," Cynthia said.

I've heard Cynthia sing at home, but never professionally. When she sings at a wedding or a birthday, I can't go because it's private, and when she sings in a club or a bar, Mom won't let me go. She says any place that serves alcohol is no place for someone my age. I've told her I'd only sit at a table and sip a glass of soda, or even water. At least, Cynthia would have *one* person truly listening. What she hates most about nightclubs is that people are there to booze and don't really care about the performers. "We're just background noise," she says.

I took the first tray of cookies out of the oven. Mom was telling Cynthia something about Mrs. Birdsall, one of the women she cleans for, when Cynthia broke in. "I've got to tell you something, Janie."

"What? Is anything wrong?" Mom sat down at

the table, clutching her hair. She does that when she gets worried.

"Not wrong. Right!" Cynthia said. "Can you guess? What do I want more than anything?"

"A million dollars."

"No, be serious. Better than that."

"Okay. A booking in a big concert hall."

"Better than that."

"Better than *that?* What could be better—" Mom said, then she broke off. "Cynthia!"

"Yes!" Cynthia said. "I just found out. Just this afternoon."

"Found out what?" I said.

"When?" Mom said.

"March," Cynthia said.

"What?" I said.

"March fifteenth," Cynthia said.

"Oh, Cynthia!" Mom put her hand to her mouth.

"Will somebody *please* tell me—"

"I'm going to have a baby," Cynthia said, turning to me. "Isn't it wonderful, Sarabeth?"

Now, here comes something not nice, but true. I didn't think it was so wonderful. First, Cynthia was too old to be having a baby, ten years older than Mom, almost forty! Besides—I know this is selfish, but I thought it—she wouldn't have time for me anymore.

"What did Billy say?" Mom asked.

"He doesn't know yet. I'll get him on the phone tonight when he's off duty."

Billy is a supply sergeant in the army. He lives on base during the week.

"He's going to be so happy," Cynthia said. "You know how much he wants a baby." She took a cigarette out of her bag.

Mom snatched at the cigarette. "Hey! You *dope!* You're pregnant now. You want to damage your baby?"

Cynthia held the cigarette out of Mom's reach— she's much taller than Mom—then dropped it into the garbage pail. "Did you see that?"

"I've seen it before," Mom said.

"No, this time it's for real. I'm through."

"And about time," Mom said. "A singer smoking! I've talked myself hoarse at you for years to do that. Throat cancer! Lung cancer!" She sat down at the table and bit her lip to keep back tears. "I always wanted another baby."

Cynthia sat down next to Mom. "Oh come on, you have enough in your life with this brat here."

"Thanks, Cynthia," I said. "I love being called a brat."

Cynthia patted her stomach. "My kid will be like a baby sister or brother to you, Sarabeth."

I didn't want to hurt her feelings by telling her thanks, but no thanks, I wasn't dying for a sister or brother. "You staying for supper?" I said. I got a can of tuna fish out of the cupboard and started mixing a casserole.

CHAPTER 6

In homeroom one day, Mr. Light started asking us questions again. "Kids, tell me three things about yourself. How many sibs you have, what your favorite food is, and what your fathers do."

Why didn't he ask about our mothers' work? Wasn't it prejudiced to ask only about fathers? It was interesting, though, to listen to what kids said. "I have two brothers, my favorite food is chunky peanut butter, my father is an insurance agent . . . two sisters, lamb chops, and my dad teaches . . . no sibs . . . my father owns United Print . . . roast beef and salami . . . one brother and one sister . . ."

When Mr. Light got to Grant, I turned around. "One sister," she said. "Pecans." She was sitting in that way she had, right in the middle of her seat, her back very straight.

"And your father's work?"

"I don't know." Her voice was even and quiet.

Mr. Light pulled his yellow sweater down over his tummy and smiled at Grant. "She doesn't know what her father does," he teased.

"My stepfather owns a tool renting company," Grant said. "I don't know what my real father does because"—she pressed her lips together, then went on—"I don't know where he is."

I could tell she hated saying it, and it made me mad at Mr. Light for asking such personal questions. When he got to me, instead of saying something about Mom's work the way I'd planned, I said the same thing Grant had said. "I don't know what my father does because I don't know where he is." And I tried to answer like her, too, quietly and evenly. I looked right at Mr. Light, telling him with my eyes that he was snooping. He went on to the next person.

At the end of the day, I was waiting for the bus when Grant came up to me. "Hi," she said. "You're Sarabeth?"

"Yes. Hi!" I suddenly felt so happy.

She hugged her books to her chest. "Do you take the bus every day?"

I nodded.

"I walk home," she said.

"I wish I did. It's a pain riding the bus, especially on a nice day, but in the winter, sometimes I'm just as glad. It's warm in the bus, and I get to do my homework. It isn't *that* awful. Sometimes it stinks a little, but the kids are okay. And I don't have to wait very long for it, usually."

I heard myself blabbing. This was the chance I'd been waiting for ever since the first day of school, and I was telling Grant everything she never wanted to know about being a bus kid. Think of something better to say, I told myself. Quick! Before she vanishes in a puff of smoke.

"Do you have a very long ride?" She sounded polite, as if she didn't really care.

"It's not that long, half an hour."

She looked away for a moment, then back at me. "Is that true about your father?"

"What? Is what true?"

"That you don't know where he is."

"Oh, that. In a way, yes. And in a way, no."

"Which one?"

"Mostly no."

"Do you lie a lot?"

My skin started burning under my eyes. "I don't lie!"

"Then why'd you say it? Were you mocking me out?"

"No! I wouldn't do that! No! That's not why I said it!"

"You said it because of me, didn't you?"

"But not that way! Not the way you think, not to mock you out. Anyway, what I said wasn't a real lie. In a way I don't know where my father is, because he's dead."

"He's dead?"

"Yes. I'm sorry."

"Why are you saying you're sorry to me?" She sounded cool and superior. She had a rich girl's voice. I knew I could never sound like that.

"I mean," I stumbled, "you don't have to feel bad for me that he's dead, because he's been dead a long time." That wasn't what I meant to say. Everything was coming out wrong. If only the bus would come and whisk me away. If only I could go back to this morning and start over again.

Then Grant said, sort of thoughtfully, "Sometimes I wonder if my father's dead. He's been gone a long time."

I felt encouraged. "You really don't know where he is?"

Her face clouded. "I don't care to talk about it." As abruptly as she had come up to me, she walked away.

CHAPTER 7

Leo doesn't walk into a house like anybody else. He bangs on the door and shouts, "It's Leo here," and then he comes in and shouts some more. "Jane? Hello! Sarabeth? Hello! Leo's here."

I was in the living room, half doing homework, half trying to make up my mind about going to the school dance. I loved to dance, but what if nobody asked me? Maybe Grant would be there, though. I would see her, I might even get to talk to her again.

I could hear Leo scraping mud off his boots on the little rug near the door. "Jane? Hello, hello!"

I closed my math book. No use trying to think with him around. Whenever Leo came over, our house seemed to get smaller. Remember that part in *Alice in Wonderland* when she drinks from the Drink

Me bottle and starts shrinking? Leo was like that bottle of Drink Me, and our trailer was like Alice, guzzling him down, drinking and shrinking.

I went into the kitchen. "Hi, Leo."

"Sarabee!" He was wearing tight faded jeans and a striped shirt with the sleeves rolled up to the shoulders so you couldn't miss the muscle show. Mom says Leo is a gorgeous guy, but to me he looks like the top half of one person stuck on the bottom half of another person. His shoulders, arms, and chest are all big, broad, and well developed, with lots of muscle. Then he suddenly narrows, tapers down to short, skinny legs. In my old school, in the front hall where I saw it every morning when I walked in, there was a framed picture of a centaur, the mythical creature who was half horse, half man. The first time I saw Leo, I thought, *Right. Centaur.* Except Leo has two legs instead of four.

He dropped a bag of groceries on the table and we shook hands. "How's the chimney business, Leo?" He's a chimney sweep.

"Starting to heat up, Sarabee."

"A ha ha ha, Leo."

"Hey, I wasn't even trying to be funny. Need another handshake?"

"I might," I said, thinking of Grant, and we shook hands again.

It's good luck to shake hands with a chimney

sweep. Right after Mom met Leo (she was cleaning a house out in the valley and he was cleaning the chimney), he came over to visit us wearing his chimney sweep clothes: black tailcoat, white neck cloth, and tall black hat. As soon as he came in, he shook Mom's hand and then mine. He shook our hands for a long time. "Now you don't have to worry about anything," he said.

And Mom said, "Oh, if it was only that simple, wouldn't the world be a nice place!"

"Where's Janie?" he said now.

"Taking a nap."

"Okay, let her sleep." He started taking things out of the grocery bag. "We're eating Middle Eastern tonight. Pita-bread sandwiches."

I examined the pita bread—six little things that looked like half-flat hats in a plastic bag. "What do you do with them?" I said.

"We heat them up until they get puffy and delicious, then we stuff them with hummus, tomatoes, avocado, sprouts—"

"Hummus? What's *hummus*, Leo?"

"Try not to be narrow-minded, Sarabeth. Hummus is *great* Middle Eastern food. Mashed chickpeas with garlic, tahini, yogurt and—"

"Ugh! It sounds horrible!" I looked out the window. It was already dark, but I could see the Goldmobile glittering. "Leo, how come you drove the Goldmobile?"

"Maybe Jane and I will go for a ride."

Normally, Leo drove a black panel truck with a picture of a chimney sweep painted on it. The Goldmobile was his special vehicle, not for every day. The first time I saw it, I didn't know what I was looking at—something shining and bristling like a huge, spiky, gorgeous monster.

When I got closer I saw that it was a van, every inch of it covered with brass objects. Angels and eagles, unicorns, deer, and dogs were riveted on the doors, the hood, the fenders, and the roof. I walked all around it, around and around. Trees, pots, trays, bells, pans, panthers, frogs, bugs, and tigers, all of them shimmering like gold.

Before it became the Goldmobile, it was an old faded green van that someone was junking. Leo was fourteen years old when he bought it. He didn't have any special plans for it, he just wanted a van.

"Then," he told Mom and me, "one of those things happened, the kind of thing that can change your life. I was walking home from school and I saw a brass lion's-head door knocker on someone's trash. I took it home, cleaned it up, and polished it. And then I got the idea of riveting it onto the door of the van.

"My father laughed. A door knocker on a truck! My mom and my brothers all thought it was hilarious. The 'knock-knock' jokes never stopped. So I found a brass ashtray in a junk store, and I cleaned that up and riveted it on the other door—to give them something else to make jokes about.

"Next it was three monkeys, one with his hands over his eyes, one with his hands over his ears, one with his hands over his mouth. See no evil. Hear no evil. Speak no evil. I traded my comic-book collection for them and riveted them above the door knocker. My father said, 'You're really serious about this, aren't you?' Then my brothers got together and gave me a brass angel for my birthday. You can see her right on the front fender. Since then, well—I've just never stopped."

Leo and I were setting the table when Mom came out of the bedroom. Her eyes were a little puffy from her nap, but she had put on her good yellow shirt and fresh eye makeup.

"Did I wake you up?" Leo said.

Mom yawned. "Sort of, but I was sleeping too long, anyway." She gave him a smile.

"Did you work today?" he asked.

"Are you kidding? Washing windows." She yawned again. "How about you?"

"Still slow. Another month, though, and all these people who forget the cold weather is coming will all want their chimneys cleaned at the same time. . . . I was done at noon today."

"That's the life." Mom leaned against him. "You brought food. Anything good?"

"Everything good."

"Hummus!" I said. "I may go to bed hungry tonight."

Leo started slicing tomatoes and giving orders. "Put the pita in a warm oven, Jane. Sprouts in a bowl, Sarabeth. You have any lettuce?"

We got everything out on the table and sat down for supper. For a while, we were busy fixing our sandwiches. They didn't taste too bad.

"Mom," I said, "should I go to the school dance tonight?"

"Hon, it's up to you."

"Leo, should I go to the school dance tonight?"

"Yes."

"Why?"

"Why not?"

"Because I don't know anybody."

"Go, Sarabeth."

"Give me one good reason."

"I'll give you two. First, because I say so and I'm older and that means I'm smarter. And second, if you don't try things, you won't ever know."

"Know what?"

"Know what might have happened." He looked at Mom. "Take Jane and me. If I hadn't talked to her that day—"

"You didn't talk to me," Mom said. "I talked to you."

"Take hummus and pita bread. If you never tried it, how would you know how good it is? You like it, right?"

"Overall, yes."

"There you go," Leo said. He made another sandwich and put it on Mom's plate. "Eat up, Janie. If you want me to marry you, you have to put a little meat on those bones. Did you know your mother proposed to me, Sarabeth?"

I put down my sandwich. Would Mom do something like that without telling me?

"Leo," Mom said.

"She begged me to marry her. You should have heard her. Promised to take care of me, all sorts of stuff."

"*Leo,*" Mom said again.

He smiled and smoothed back his hair. It's silky brownish. He wears it slicked back, flat and shiny. "I'm definitely thinking about it, because I know we'd have really cute babies."

My cheeks got hot. Mom had said she wanted another baby. My heart thumped hard. Leo, my *father?* I looked at him. I thought, *Leo has such irritating hair.* And suddenly I reached over and ruffled his hair, messing it around and mussing it up.

"Hey!" he said, dropping his spoon.

"Hey!" I said back, mussing up his hair some more.

"Sarabeth, what are you doing?" Mom said.

"Quit it," he said.

I started jumping around and really going after Leo's hair. He tried to hold me off, putting out his arms, first to one side, then the other. I kept after him, jumping and pouncing.

"Sarabeth," Mom said. "Will you please leave Leo alone!"

"She's having an adolescent glandular fit," Leo said.

I sat down and folded my napkin.

"Look at that girl." Leo pushed his hair back into place, all slick and shiny. "Look at her."

I stared down at the table. What a dumb thing to do! I felt sort of ashamed, but I also felt happier, lighter and freer. And Leo's hair didn't irritate me anymore. "Mom, did you ask Leo to marry you?"

"Sure she did," Leo said.

"Le-o!" Mom said.

"What, *Le-o?* What? Okay, the truth. *I* asked *her,* Sarabeth."

"Serious?"

"Absolutely. Listen, I love your mom."

I sat up straight. "What did you say, Mom?"

"I said I'm not fifteen years old anymore. I said *if* I got married again, and *if* I ever had another baby, I would not be poor and do it. And then I said, it's therefore silly to talk about marriage, because Leo has even less money than we do!"

Leo leaned on his elbow and blew out his breath.

"You forgot to tell Sarabeth one thing, Jane. You forgot to say how I'm too young for you. The *biiig* five years."

"Right. The *biiig* five years," Mom said.

"You know, I've figured out something really important. I'm always going to be five years younger than you."

"Right. I'm older and smarter. Quote, unquote, Leo."

"That's why I want to marry you. I need somebody smart in my life. When we're married, you're the boss. I'll write it into the vows. Love, honor, and obey. I'll get up there and say it."

"Leo, no more tonight," Mom said.

He snapped out a salute. "I hear and I obey!"

"Boy, sometimes you vex me," Mom said.

"I do?"

"Yeah, you do."

"Mom, not *yeah*," I said. *"Yes."*

"Oh, between the two of you—!" Mom pushed back her chair.

Leo looked at me. "We'll behave. Right, Sarabeth?"

"Right, Leo."

"We won't say another word. Right, Sarabeth?"

"Right, Leo."

Mom brought the ice cream to the table. "Eat up and shut up, kiddies."

CHAPTER 8

Mom drove me to school. I sat in the backseat, behind Leo. The building was lit up, and kids were going in. Mom checked her watch. "We'll pick you up after the movie, around ten. You wait outside, okay?" She patted her cheek. "Lay one on me right here."

I kissed her. "What if nobody asks me to dance, Mom?"

"Then you ask them," Leo said.

"The girl can't ask," Mom said.

"Oh, come on, Janie," Leo said. "Sure she can."

"I could *never* ask a guy to dance," I said.

"Sure you could, Sarabee."

"Maybe I'll go to the movies with you guys, after all."

"Go to the dance," Leo said. He turned around to look at me. "You are not going to be sorry."

"Leo, what if I have a stinking, lousy time?"

"Sarabeth, you're not the sort of person who has a stinking, lousy time anywhere."

"How do you know that?"

"You're the sort of person who, even when she's going somewhere that she doesn't know anybody, is going to make sure she has at least an *okay* time. Maybe not the greatest time in the world, but definitely an *okay* time."

"You want to get rid of me so you can be alone with Mom."

"True. But I also mean every word." He reached over and mussed up my hair.

"Leo! Look what you did to my hair!"

"Revenge, Sarabeth."

"That is really childish," Mom said.

"Don't get mad at Leo," I said. "I had it coming."

"You sure did, you little creep." Leo pulled out his comb and handed it to me. I fixed my hair and looked in the mirror. "You look pretty," he said. "I like your dress."

I was wearing a yellow cotton dress with a flared skirt and spaghetti straps. Mom and I bought it in the Rescue Mission for two dollars. It was really for summer but it was the nicest dress I had. "Mom, do I look all right?"

She pushed my hair off my forehead. "You're fine. Let me see your hands. Are they clean?"

I hid my thumbs in my palms. "Mom! She thinks I'm five years old," I said to Leo as I got out of the car.

Mom leaned out the window. "Sarabeth, are you okay? Will you be okay, hon?"

"Of course she's okay," Leo said.

Something about the way he was looking at me and laughing made me laugh, too. "I hope the movie isn't a dog," I said. I walked toward the gym.

Inside, kids were dancing and going to the refreshment table and standing around in groups. I didn't see anybody I recognized, and I didn't see anyone else alone. I walked around, checking people out, as if I were looking for someone and thinking impatiently, *Well, where is she? Where is my friend?* That worked pretty well until something else started bothering me. *What if the girl who used to own my dress is here?*

I glanced around at different girls, trying not to be too obvious, to see who was the same size as me. I was afraid someone would stop me and say, "I used to have a dress just like that. Same color, same spaghetti straps, same everything. I gave it away to the Rescue Mission with a lot of other old junk."

On my second time around the gym, I saw Grant. She was with Jennifer, Patty, and Asa. They were talking and laughing, joking around with some older boys. They were all wearing gold hoop earrings and Kelly-green blouses, as if they belonged to a club. Exclusive club. One that didn't include Sarabeth Silver and wasn't ever going to include Sarabeth Silver.

I walked away. A moment later, I noticed something else. How had I missed it? Every girl in the room was wearing cords with the cuffs rolled up, high tops, and white ankle socks. Everything I was wearing was wrong. The yellow dress. My sandals. Mom's ceramic earrings. Wrong, all wrong!

I went over to the refreshment table. I took a cup of punch and drank it fast. Then another cup. A short, chubby girl was nearby. I hoped I didn't look like her! She was dressed right, cords and high tops and everything, but she looked as if she were on the verge of crying.

"Hi," I said.

"Hi." She gave me a wobbly smile.

"I'm Sarabeth Silver."

"Frankie Klematis."

"Frankie? Is that short for anything?"

"No, that's my original name."

I held up my cup. "Good punch."

"Really." She gave me another wobbly smile.

We walked around together, drinking punch. I told her I had just transferred to DSD. "Really?" she said. I told her about my old school, how the teachers there were so much more buttoned down. "Really!" she said. I did most of the talking. I didn't mind. It was great having someone to talk to. Then a boy came up and asked Frankie to dance.

She looked at me. "I'm going to get some more punch," I said. So then she went out on the floor with him. I checked the time. Only seven-thirty, hours to go before Mom came for me.

I drank two more cups of punch and checked the time again. Seven forty-five. Frankie Klematis was still dancing with the same boy. She looked pretty happy now. Was that because she liked the boy or because she was *with* a boy? I decided I would be happy if a boy asked me to dance *only* if I liked him.

Jennifer and Asa were dancing with each other. They went right by me. It was a hot beat, and Asa's face was red and sweaty and smiling. They looked cute dancing together because they were so different, Jennifer, skinny and redheaded. Asa, plump and dark.

I circled the gym again and wound up standing near the scoreboard. A boy with curly hair drifted over. He was wearing a T-shirt that said SAVE THE WHALES with a picture below of a whale leaping out of water. He smiled. Braces and large teeth, sort of rabbity-looking. I smiled back. "Hi."

"Hi."

"I'm Sarabeth Silver."

"Mark Emelsky."

It was like the conversation with Frankie Klematis all over again. The next thing I said was, "I'm new in this school."

"Me, too. Sort of."

At least he didn't say *Really!* There was something about him I liked. Maybe it was that rabbity look, sincere and nice. I said, "Now that we know each other, maybe we should say hello again."

"That's a good idea. Hello, Sarabeth!"

"Hello, Mark," I said. "Imagine meeting you here!" Then I thought, I've gone this far, I might as well go all the way, or as Mom says, "In for a penny, in for a pound." And I asked him to dance.

CHAPTER 9

"Sarabeth, I have something to tell you," Mark said while we were dancing. "I don't go to this school. I go to Persian Stone Ridge."

"The private school? You must be really rich." I was afraid that sounded rude, but Mark didn't seem to mind.

"My mother teaches there, so I get to go tuition-free."

"Do you like it?"

"It's an okay school. I'm getting a good education."

"Don't they have dances over there?"

"They do, but I know kids from this school so I decided to come here for a change. A friend from Persian was going to meet me, but he didn't show up. Lucky for me," he added, giving me a really nice smile.

"So why do the whales have to be saved?" I said, pointing to his T-shirt. "Or is that a joke?"

"No joke. Whales are an endangered species. One of thousands of endangered species—maybe even millions—but they're my special interest. I'm fascinated by whales. They're kind, intelligent, and gentle. They're some of the biggest creatures on earth, but they don't hurt anybody. We hurt them. . . . Oh, sorry, is this boring you?"

"No, it's interesting."

"Some people, like my older sister, are always telling me not to be so serious, to lighten up."

"Why? Because you like whales?"

"She thinks I take everything too seriously. She says life is for fun, not for moaning over. I don't think I *moan* over things, but I guess I do get bothered by stuff. Do you know, Sarabeth, that all over the world we're losing species at the rate of at least one a day? Some scientists say that in a hundred years, we'll have lost nine million species."

"Nine million?" I said.

"Not nine million animals. Nine million *species.*"

"I can't even imagine a number like that," I said.

"I know what you mean. It depresses me to think about it. It's not so bad when you concentrate on just one family of animals, like whales. Then you can try to help save them. Do you know that whales sing, Sarabeth?"

"I've heard of that. Is it like the way we sing?"

"It's totally different. It's eerie and beautiful."

"I suppose it's their way of talking to each other."

Mark nodded. "Someday if you come over to my house, I'll play you a whale-songs record."

"Where do you live?"

"Hickory Street. Where do you live?"

"Roadview Trailer Park."

"Huh!" he said.

Jennifer and her dumb remarks about bathrooms and winter jumped into my mind. *"Huh?"* I repeated. "What does that mean?"

"Nothing, I'm just surprised. I don't know anybody who lives in a trailer park."

"And so?"

"So nothing. It's interesting."

I was annoyed. I didn't see what was so "interesting" about living in Roadview. Did he think people who lived in trailer parks were an endangered species? I opened my mouth to say something, but just then we almost bumped into Grant. She was dancing with an older boy. She gave Mark a long look, then she turned to me and smiled. "Hi, Sarabeth!"

I was so surprised by her friendliness I almost didn't answer. "Hi, Grant," I said finally.

"Having a good time?" she asked.

"Oh . . . yes."

"Great!" She gave me an approving look and danced away.

"Wasn't that Grant Varrow?" Mark said. "I knew her in second grade. We went to the same school. I guess she didn't recognize me."

"I guess not." I twisted around to see Grant again. *Hi, Sarabeth! Great that you're having a good time!* Said as if she were my dearest friend!

"Did you ever hear of Shana Emelsky?" Mark was saying.

"I don't think so. Should I have?"

"Just if you read the sports pages. She's my older sister. Last spring she won the State Junior Women's Tennis Tournament. My mother was an athlete in college. She taught my sister to play tennis when Shana was three years old."

"That's young, isn't it?"

"Mom and Dad got her a special little racket. Shana's a natural."

"Are you good at sports, too?"

"I ski, but that's all. And I play a little tennis. My father, my little sister Kate and I are all pretty much the same, not great athletes like my mother and Shana. . . . You want something to drink, Sarabeth? I'm thirsty."

We went over to the refreshment table. "My treat," Mark said. He bought two orange sodas and we walked around with our sodas, talking. Mark told me he was a vegetarian. "Ever since I got interested in animals, I stopped liking meat."

"I love meat," I said.

"I did, too. I was your regular happy carnivore. Then I started thinking how meat comes from something that was a living being. I found out that chickens don't just topple over and die. They're murdered. Someone slits their throats, or a machine does it. To me, that's even worse. Do you know that cows are smashed in the head, and they cry when it's going to happen? They seem to know they're going to be killed."

"No, stop," I said.

"And veal—you know what that is? That's baby meat. It comes from calves, that's why it's so tender. They never even get to grow up. After I read that, I didn't want meat anymore."

I shuddered. "That's awful, but I don't know if I could give up meat. I don't think I could. What do you eat? Aren't you hungry?"

"There are plenty of things. I had tofu burgers for supper tonight."

"What's tofu?" It sounded awful, like something Leo would like.

"It's soybean curd. Sort of like white cheese. You can make lots of stuff with it. You know what I like? Tofu ravioli! No, really, it's good. What'd you have for supper—a red, bloody steak?" Mark blushed. It was cute. "Oh, sorry! That was mean. Shana says I'm a boring fanatic about this stuff."

Shana was the one who was always telling him to lighten up. The tennis champ. I decided I probably wouldn't like her. "Mark, guess what? I had pita sandwiches with hummus and sprouts for supper." I laughed at his flabbergasted look and told him about Leo.

He had finished his soda. "Do you want the rest of mine?" I handed him the can. "Don't worry, I didn't drool or spit in it."

He tipped up the can. "I hope no one else asks you to dance, Sarabeth."

"If they do, I'll turn them down." I said it, but I didn't have a chance to prove it—no one else asked me. I didn't care. I was having a great time with Mark. Still, every now and then Grant popped into my mind. I couldn't figure her out. Cool and indifferent for so long, then suddenly starting to talk to me at the bus stop but misunderstanding everything. And now, tonight, so open and friendly. The three faces of Grant!

Mr. Trumpour, the principal, got up on the stage and clapped his hands. "Ladies and gentlemen, thank you for coming to our dance. You behaved perfectly. It was a great dance. We're proud of you all." Kids started cheering. Mr. Trumpour held up his hands for quiet. "We're going to have one last dance, and then it's time to depart. See you all Monday."

"Maybe I should go outside," I said. "My mom will be coming for me in a few minutes." Mark walked out with me. "Are you waiting for anyone?" I asked.

"No, I can walk home from here. It's only three blocks."

I saw our car—I should say I heard it—clanking down the street. "Here comes Mom now."

"How old is your car?" Mark asked.

"Ten years old." I could see the "Huh!" coming on his lips. "It's rusty," I said quickly, "but it runs fine. We don't care what it looks like. For us, a car is just something you use to get from one place to another, from here to there." I didn't say we didn't have the money for a new car and we weren't likely to ever have it. I didn't say that when Mom and I made up wish lists, a new car was always right on top of Mom's list, and pretty high on mine, too.

Mom honked. *Baap, baap, baap!* We have a really weird horn. I'd know it anywhere.

"Goodbye, Mark," I said. "I had fun."

"Me, too, Sarabeth." He started to walk away, then he turned and came back. "What's your phone number?" I told him and he wrote it on the back of his hand. Then we said goodbye again.

When I got in the car, Mom and Leo both

looked at me with smiles on their faces. "Who was that?" Mom said.

"A friend."

"Oh, a friend," Leo said in a teasing voice.

"Yes, Leo. A friend."

"A boyfriend, Sarabee?"

"A friend, Leo," I said, leaning over the front seat and tapping him on the shoulder. "A boy who is a friend, Leo, dear."

CHAPTER 10

Saturday morning it was raining and I stayed in bed reading a book called *My Brother Stevie*. It's one of my favorite books. I've read it at least six times. I wish it had a picture of the author on it. Eleanor Clymer. "I bet she's beautiful," I said to Tobias.

I could hear Mom talking on the phone in the kitchen. "I fell behind that week I had the flu. I thought I'd be able to pay everything anyway. . . ."

It was cozy lying there reading with Tobias warm on my stomach, and Mom's voice and the rain on the roof like background music. I was hungry but I didn't even want to get out of bed.

"And now the car needs a new muffler," Mom was saying. "And remember, Cynthia, when I had that trouble with my wisdom teeth? I still owe him a hundred. I figure I need it for about a month. Maybe six weeks, at most—"

Suddenly I realized she was talking about borrowing money. I sat up, dumping Tobias on the floor. He leaped onto the windowsill, his ears stiff with annoyance.

I went down the hall to the kitchen.

"Hi, hon," Mom said. "Hungry? Want some French toast?" She took eggs from the refrigerator. "I have just about enough time to make you a batch before I go." She was dressed for work in jeans, a sweat shirt, and sneakers. Her eyes were red.

"Mom, were you crying? Your eyes look terrible."

"It's that cold of mine, it's hanging on." She opened the egg carton.

"I'll do that," I said. I cracked an egg into a bowl and got a loaf of bread from the bread box. "I heard you talking to Cynthia. How much are we borrowing?"

"Sarabeth, were you listening? I thought you were asleep."

"I wasn't."

She filled her coffee cup and sat down at the table. "You weren't supposed to hear that."

"You know what, Mom? First you don't tell me Leo asked you to marry him. And now you don't want me to know about needing money." I whipped the eggs around with a fork. "What else aren't you telling me?"

"Hon! Nothing. I don't keep things from you."

"Yes you do, Mom! You're always saying, 'It's you and me, Sarabeth, we're a team.' But you didn't tell me we owed money. How much do we owe? We can pay our rent, can't we?"

She fixed her barrettes and pushed her hair behind her ears. "We don't owe a tremendous amount, Sarabeth. It's just . . . I guess I'm scared of really falling behind. You know, if you don't pay bills on time, they give you a late charge, so then you owe them more. At least Cynthia doesn't care if I'm late paying her."

The rain suddenly started to come down hard, the lights flickered, and it got as dark as night outside. Mom went to the window and looked out at the cliff. "I hope we don't have a landslide," she said. "Sarabeth, if it keeps raining like this, maybe you should go over to Cynthia's."

"How much do we need?" I asked again.

"What . . . ? Oh. You don't have to know that. Don't worry about it, hon."

"Mom, I wish you wouldn't say that." I dropped a slice of bread into the egg. "Don't exclude me."

Mom was quiet for a moment, looking out the window. Then she turned to me and said, "Sarabeth,

I don't want you to grow up too fast. I'm so afraid for you sometimes."

"Of what?"

Mom raised her shoulders. "Just—things. Things in general."

"Are you afraid I'll get pregnant when I'm fifteen? You are, aren't you! I'm not going to have sex when I'm just a kid, Mom. It was different for you. You didn't know about birth control when you were growing up, you told me so. We have health classes in school and I know all that stuff."

She still looked sad, so I said, "Even if I fell in love with somebody wonderful like my father, I wouldn't get pregnant. I'm not going to have sex until I'm twenty-one." I put the French toast on a plate and sat down. "I thought about it and I decided, so you can stop worrying."

"Well, stick to it," she said. "Stick to what you believe in, hon, with all your might. That's your best hope in life, because things are going to happen that have nothing to do with anything."

I knew she was talking about my father getting killed.

She sat down again and sipped her coffee. "You can plan only so much. I'm not saying planning is bad. It's good! But, still, you have to be flexible. I found that out. Sometimes there's nothing you can do, just let the stream carry you along."

We sat there for a while. Then I said, "Mom, do you want the last piece of French toast?"

Mom shook her head. "My practical Sarabeth! You're right, back to the real world." She got up and took her tote bag off the hook. "I'll be at the Reitells' on Haverford Drive. I wish I didn't have to work on Saturday and leave you—"

"Mom, you always say that and you always work on Saturday."

"Well, she asked me and I didn't want to turn her down. . . . Try and get your homework done, Sarabeth. Don't wait until the last minute." She put on her raincoat. "I promised Mrs. Louis I'd serve at her cocktail party tonight, too, so I'll be a little late."

My stomach jumped. "Who?"

"She's a new customer. At least I don't have to wear a uniform for her party. She said a dark dress would be okay." Mom checked her tote bag. "Oh, gosh, I almost forgot my black shoes."

"You said Lewis? How do they spell their name?"

"L-O-U-I-S. Why?"

"You sure it's spelled that way?"

"Of course I'm sure. I wrote it down." She got her shoes, kissed me and left.

I finished eating and took my dishes to the sink. What if it had been the way Patty spelled her name?

L-E-W-I-S. What if it had been Patty's mother giving the cocktail party? I imagined Mom parking our rusty car in front of the Lewis house. They probably lived in a huge expensive place with an enormous green lawn. Maybe it had pillars like a Southern mansion. When Patty heard the serving maid's name was Mrs. Silver, would she think of me?

"So what?" I said out loud. So what if my mother had to serve at her mother's cocktail party? Perversely, I started wishing it really was Patty's house Mom was going to. Then Patty could mention it to Grant, and the two big, rich snobs could *oooh* and *aaah* in astonishment over it.

With Mom gone, the trailer was quiet. "Tobias!" I called. He came strolling in. "Are you hungry?" I put food in his dish and turned on the radio.

The announcer said, "Be sure and take your umbrella when you go out."

"Thanks," I said, "I will."

I washed the dishes and let Tobias out. I dried the dishes and let Tobias in. I looked up "Emelsky" in the phone book. There were two Emelskys, R. R. and Peter. R. R. Emelsky lived in North Matonville. Peter Emelsky lived on Hickory Street. That must be Mark's father.

I thought about calling Mark. Should I? Or shouldn't I? I couldn't make up my mind.

He had my phone number. *He* should call *me*. I had been the one to start everything else. I had spoken first, I had asked his name, and I had asked him to dance.

I took a shower and washed my hair. I wrapped a towel around my head, turban-fashion, the way Mom did.

Then I called Cynthia. "Hi, it's me."

"Hi, darling. What's up?"

"Cynthia, I want to get a job."

"How come?"

"I want to make some money. You know—to help out. I'm old enough."

She didn't argue with me or tell me not to worry about things. "You want some suggestions? I have one idea right away for you. Do you know the Vander Burghs in Thirty-Three? They have a new baby. Maybe Laurie Vander Burgh could use a baby-sitter."

"Do you think she'd hire me?"

"I think she'd be lucky to get you."

"Should I go over there, phone her, or what?"

"Go right over, Sarabeth. Let Mrs. Vander Burgh see what kind of person you are. That's the best reference in the world."

I sat down with a piece of paper and figured out how many hours I could work and what I should make for each hour. Then I put on my slicker and walked over to the Vander Burghs'. It was still raining.

Laurie Vander Burgh came to the door. She had blonde bangs hanging in her eyes. "Yes?" she said. She was wearing short pants and a striped blue-and-white shirt with the sleeves pushed up.

"I'm Sarabeth Silver? I live in Two? Over there?" Everything I said came out like a question, maybe because I was feeling sort of anxious. "I was just wondering, um—? I heard you had a baby? I thought you might need a baby-sitter."

"Well, no, I don't." She had big lips that twisted when she spoke.

"Oh. I'm really disappointed!"

"I'm sorry," she said. "Do you like babies so much?"

"I don't think so," I said. "I was hoping to make money."

"Well, that's honest, anyway. Would you like to see my baby?"

"Sure." I took off my slicker and followed her to the baby's room. It was hot and smelled like sour milk and baby powder.

The baby was sleeping in a crib, making tiny snoring noises. It was under a white blanket embroidered with rabbits and flowers. Poking out of the top of the blanket were a little dab of black hair and tiny, bunched-up fists.

Mrs. Vander Burgh leaned over the crib. "Some

babies," she said in a hushed voice, "you can't tell what they are, boy or girl, unless they're dressed in blue or pink."

I'd never thought about that. I looked closely at the baby. I couldn't tell if it was a boy or a girl. I glanced around the room for a clue. Everything was yellow. *Boy,* I thought.

"And of course you never want to say to a mother her baby is a boy when it's a girl," Mrs. Vander Burgh went on.

"Oh, no," I agreed. Did that mean her baby was a girl?

"I used to think it didn't make any difference. A baby is a baby, isn't it? That's what I thought until I had my own little Jerry." She laughed. "Now I'm like all the mothers. I'd hate for anyone to make a mistake with my little darling."

Jerry. Boy, for sure.

Mrs. Vander Burgh stroked the baby's tiny head. "I know every mother says this, but isn't she beautiful?"

"Oh, *she* is," I said with relief. "How do you spell her name?"

"G-E-R-I. It's short for Geraldine. Isn't that a beautiful old-fashioned name?"

I touched Geri's head. "So soft," I said. I touched one of her little fists, and the fingers suddenly spread out.

"You know, Sarabeth," Mrs. Vander Burgh

said, "what I really need is someone to help me clean up this place. Everything's gotten into such a mess since Geri was born. I guess you're too young for that kind of work, though."

"I know how to clean. You could just tell me what you want and I'll do it."

"I couldn't pay you very much. I mean, not as much as I would pay a woman."

"Whatever you can pay would be all right."

"Well . . . when would you start?"

"Right now."

"Wonderful!" When she smiled, you didn't notice her big twisty lips or the way her hair hung in her eyes.

The house really was messy. Dishes in the sink and baby clothes hanging everywhere. "I just haven't been able to do anything, Sarabeth," Mrs. Vander Burgh kept saying.

After a while, when Geri woke up, I could see why. It seemed as if every two minutes her mother had to do something else for Geri—feed her, burp her, change her, pick her up, walk her around, give her a bath, feed her again. And Geri was really smart! The minute Mrs. Vander Burgh tried to do anything that didn't involve her, Geri started fretting. "Here I am," Mrs. Vander Burgh said, rushing over to her, and Geri thumped her legs.

I worked all afternoon—mainly washing dishes

and vacuuming. When I went home, I lay down on my bed. I was going to read, but I must have fallen asleep. I woke up when I heard Mom calling, "Sarabeth? Why are the lights off?"

I staggered into the kitchen. The rain was beating down on the roof. "Did you just get home, Mom? What time is it?"

"Eight o'clock." She dropped into a chair and kicked off her shoes. "I am totally bushed. Oh, my poor feet." She massaged her toes. "Get me a pan of hot water, hon. . . . What'd you have for supper?"

"I didn't eat yet, Mom." I took the money I'd earned out of my jeans and put it on the table. "Mom, that's for you."

"What is it?"

"What *is* it? It's money, Mom!"

"I mean, what's it for? Where'd it come from?"

"I earned it, cleaning for Mrs. Vander Burgh."

"You did what?"

"Mom, Mrs. Vander Burgh in Thirty-Three just had a baby, and she really needs help. I was there all afternoon, and she wants me to come in next—"

I never got to finish my sentence. Mom smacked me across the face. "You were cleaning house? Who gave you permission? I forbid you to do that. Do you hear me? I forbid you!"

I stood there in shock. My cheek stung. I could

hardly breathe. "The money's for you," I got out.

She pushed it off the table. She kicked it away from her. "I don't want that money! Just because I clean houses, you're going to do it? No, you aren't! I will not have it! What a stupid, stupid, *stupid* thing for you to do."

My eyes were hot. "I didn't do anything wrong. I worked and earned some money to help us out."

The phone rang. We both looked at it. "Get it," Mom said.

I went to the door. The phone kept ringing.

"Sarabeth," Mom said. "Sarabeth!"

I didn't answer her. I didn't stop. I walked out.

CHAPTER 11

I ran. It was raining harder than ever. Lights were on everywhere. I ran past the Vander Burghs' trailer and then the Kralls' trailer. Through their front window, I saw Mr. and Mrs. Munge sitting at a table, playing cards. No one looked out. No one saw me. I ran across Rock Road and climbed up the embankment onto the shoulder of the interstate. The gray shapes of cars sped past, rain falling like needles into their yellow headlights.

I put out my thumb and, like magic, a car stopped. A woman leaned out. "Where do you want to go?" she asked.

"Hickory Street." I said the first thing I thought of.

"Get in."

I climbed in and shut the door. I was shivering. A little pool of water formed around my feet.

"What are you doing way out here?" she said. She didn't start driving. "Do you know how dangerous hitchhiking is? Where do you live?"

I pointed over my shoulder.

"What's over there?"

"Roadview."

"What?" She frowned. "Speak up, child!"

"Roadview Trailer Park!"

She peered through the window. "Those lights?"

I nodded.

"Where's your mother?" she said. "Do you know I could call the police and tell them you're out here hitchhiking? I bet you aren't more than twelve years old."

"I'm almost fourteen!"

"Wonderful. Congratulations on being so stupid at such a young age."

I couldn't believe this was happening to me. I couldn't believe that Mom had slapped me, that this stranger was yelling at me, that twice in the last hour I'd been called stupid.

"I'm driving you home," she said. "I'm making sure your mother knows what you've been up to."

"No!" I opened the door.

She grabbed my arm. "Where do you think

you're going? The only place you're going is home, where you belong."

"Okay, okay!"

"No, not *okay, okay,*" she mimicked. "You're to go home!"

"I will," I said. I opened the door so fast I almost fell out of the car.

She leaned across the seat. "I'm not moving from here. I'm watching you. Go home, and don't ever hitchhike again. Go on," she said, like I was a dog. "Go on, right now!"

I climbed back over the fence and ran and slid down the muddy embankment. At the bottom, on Rock Road, I looked back. I could see her headlights veering off at an angle in the rain. I crossed the road and looked back again. She was still there.

I went to Cynthia's house. It was dim, just one little light on. I knocked, but nobody answered.

I opened the door. I heard someone singing. "Cynthia?" I called. Then I realized it was a record, Linda Ronstadt. "Cynthia? Anybody home?" I walked toward the living room and stumbled over a wooden box on the floor near the piano. *"Ouuwww."* I was breathing hard, holding back tears.

Billy and Cynthia came down the hall. They must have been in bed. Billy was pulling on a sweater over pj bottoms, and Cynthia was tying her robe. Her hair was long and loose around her shoulders. "Sarabeth?" she said. She put her arm around me and walked me toward the table. There were candles on the table and supper dishes. "Sarabeth, you're soaked! What have you been doing?"

I stared at her, blinking and shivering.

"Your mom called," Billy said. "Do you know she's looking for you?" He pulled out a chair. "Sit down, kiddo." He started drying my hair with a napkin.

I bent my head and closed my eyes. I breathed in the smell of candles and meat and something spicy and hot. I wanted to thank Billy for drying my hair. I wanted to tell him it was good he was a supply sergeant—in charge of shoes and sheets and things like that—because he wouldn't last two seconds as a drill sergeant. At least not according to the movie I'd seen on TV, where the drill sergeant was always cursing and beating up the soldiers and forcing them to march around all night with eighty-pound packs on their backs.

Billy sat on one side of me and Cynthia on the other. She took my hand. "Well, Sarabeth?"

I still didn't speak. It seemed like the most impossible thing in the world to say anything. All these things were going through my mind. Billy . . . Mom . . . Mrs. Vander Burgh . . . Geri . . . money . . . that woman on the interstate. I stared at Cynthia's robe. There was a little rip in the corner of the pocket.

"Are you hungry?" Billy asked.

I shook my head.

"Why don't we get you a change of clothes," Cynthia said. "Then we can talk."

I followed her into the bedroom. Their trailer was smaller than ours. The bedroom was always stuffed with things—Cynthia's sewing machine, their TV and stereo, boxes of clothes and things Cynthia didn't have any place for. She gave me one of her robes to put on. It was huge and warm. It felt wonderful, and I tied the belt twice around my waist.

"Now, how about those feet?" She gave me a pair of dry socks and rolled up my wet clothes. "I'll stick these in the dryer. Come on, don't look so tragic." She hugged me. "Whatever it is, it'll be okay."

"I'm not going home," I said. I held on to her. "I'm going to stay with you and Billy. I'll sleep on the couch. I'll sleep on the floor, I don't care, I'm just not going home."

"Easy does it, Sarabeth."

In the dining room, Billy had a plate of food for me. "Eat something," he said. "It'll make you feel better."

I picked at the meat. It seemed so long ago that Mark had told me how cows cried before they were killed. I ate the peas and carrots and three pieces of garlic bread.

"What's the matter with the meat?" Billy said.

"Nothing, it's fine. I just don't want it."

"Eat a little, anyway," he urged.

"No, leave her alone, Billy," Cynthia said. "Sarabeth, I'm going to call Jane and tell her you're here."

"Cynthia, I don't want to go home!"

"Well, that's okay, but I still have to call." She went into her bedroom to use the phone.

Billy lit a cigarette. "Want to tell me what's going on?"

I shook my head. Then I said, "Mom and I had a fight."

"I figured that much out, kiddo. What was it about? Uh-oh! Look at me, look what I'm doing." He mashed his cigarette in the saucer.

"Are you trying to stop smoking because of the baby?"

"*Trying* is the operative word. I'm working on it. I'm down to half a pack a day. I'm going to beat it, though. I don't want my kid growing up with me blowing smoke into her lungs."

A few minutes later, Mom walked in. She had her raincoat flung over the top of her head. She didn't even say hello, just began ordering me around. "Sarabeth, get up, get dressed. You're coming home."

I pushed away the plate. I didn't say anything.

"Where were you?" Mom said.

I started breathing hard again.

"Your mom's talking to you," Billy said. He suddenly sounded like a drill sergeant.

"I'm not talking to her."

"In my house, kiddo, when your mother talks, you answer."

"Back off, Billy," Cynthia said. "Give her a chance." She stood behind my chair, her hands on my shoulders.

"I'm not going home," I said. "Cynthia said I can stay here. I can stay here, can't I, Cynthia?"

"Where are you going to sleep?" Mom said. "In the bathtub?"

"Oh, you're so big and smart!"

"Sarabeth!" Billy said. And then Mom and Cynthia said it. "Sarabeth!"

They were all yelling at me! I knew I was going to start crying any minute. I looked wildly around the room. I wanted to run, hide under the table, smash a dish, do something! I felt all alone. My thoughts were confused. I didn't know *what* I would do.

Then Cynthia squeezed my shoulder, squeezed it hard, and rubbed the back of my neck. That helped. I don't know why, but it did. Her fingers seemed to be telling me it was okay, she loved me, she wasn't really mad at me.

I slumped down. I didn't want to look at anyone. They all started talking. Mom wanted me to go home. Billy said I should, too. But Cynthia said my clothes were still in the dryer. "Why don't you and Sarabeth go into my bedroom and talk?" she said to Mom. "You can be as private as you want there. And meanwhile, Billy and I will clean up this mess. Won't we, Sarge?"

They all laughed, as if nothing was the matter. I got up and followed Mom into the bedroom. She shut the door. "Where did you go, Sarabeth?"

I pointed toward the window.

"What's over there?"

"The road."

"Rock Road?"

"No."

"The highway?"

"Yes."

"What were you doing out there?"

"Hitchhiking."

"Hitchhiking? Sarabeth, what's the matter with you? You know better than that."

"What's the matter with *you?*" I said. "You hit me. You hit me on the face!" I started to cry. "You don't even care."

"How can you say that? Come on, let's make up." Mom tried to hug me. I stood stiffly, my arms at my sides. "You don't want to make up?"

"No, not with you." Then Mom started to cry,

too. That's one thing I can't stand. "Stop crying!" I said.

"I'm not crying; I never cry."

"You're crying!"

"So are you."

"Well, I have a good reason. You don't love me."

Mom sat down hard on the bed. "I don't love you? I can't even breathe when you say a thing like that." She stared at me. "If I don't love you, then what am I doing here on earth?" Her eyes were wet, and I started to feel ashamed and sad.

"Come over here," she said after a moment. She tapped the bed, and I sat down next to her. "Put your arms around me." I did, and she put her arms around me. "Hug me," she said. "Harder." She hugged me back, hugged me tight. "Now tell me I don't love you," she said.

I didn't say anything. I put my head on her shoulder. I was glad we were sitting down, because that way I didn't tower over her.

"Let me see your cheek," she said. "Did I leave a mark?" She smoothed her hand over my face. "I don't know what got into me. The idea of you cleaning house just drove me wild. I want something better for you."

"You're the one who always says housework is honest work, there's no disgrace in honest work.

And then when I—" My voice went wobbly.

"I know, I know. You're right. Try to understand. . . . I can't bear the thought that you won't have a wonderful life. I want you to have a better life than I do."

"What's wrong with our life? Don't you think we have a nice life?"

"I want more for you, Sarabeth. I have dreams for you. I want you to finish high school and go to college. I want you to have an education and a profession, to be something, maybe a doctor. Would you like that?"

"Dr. Sarabeth Silver," I said. "Calling Dr. Silver."

Mom smiled. "That sounds all right to me."

Cynthia knocked and walked in. She was yawning. "You two wrapped things up yet?"

"Cynthia, do you think I should go to cooking school or medical school?"

"That's an interesting choice."

"Maybe I'll do both."

"Who's going to pay for all this?"

"Me," I said, looking at Mom. "I'll save the money I make working for Mrs. Vander Burgh."

CHAPTER 12

"Hi, Sarabeth." Grant was standing by my desk when I walked into homeroom.

"Hi," I said. And I remained standing. I didn't want to sit down. I didn't want to be lower than Grant, looking up at her. Which was exactly what I'd been doing for weeks—looking up at Grant, looking up to her.

"Remember at the bus last week, when we were talking about your father and my father?" Grant said.

"I remember." I folded my arms.

"Well, I've been thinking—"

Mr. Light rapped on his desk. "I have a few announcements. Grant, would you sit down, please?

Randy. Beverly. You people over there in the back of the room—"

"Talk to you later, okay?" Grant said.

I didn't see her again until lunchtime. She was at a table with her three pals, as usual. She waved to me to come over. I walked slowly across the room. She made a place for me next to her, and I sat down on the edge of the bench.

"Hi," Jennifer said, through a mouthful of food.

Patty glanced up briefly. She was wearing pink earrings, pink nail polish. One strand of her shining blonde hair was braided with a pink satin ribbon.

"Oh hello, Sarabeth Silver," Asa said, giving me an intense look. She had huge brown eyes.

"How'd you like the dance Friday night?" Grant asked me.

"It was okay. I like dancing." I unwrapped my sandwich carefully. Sometimes we use the wax paper twice.

"You should have seen Sarabeth dance," Grant said. "She's good!"

"Who were you dancing with?" Asa asked.

"Just a guy. A vegetarian. He won't eat meat."

Jennifer snorted. "What's that supposed to make him, a saint?"

"He doesn't like killing," I said. I turned to

Asa. "Did you ace the test?" Mr. Pelter had sprung a test on us that morning on the short story we'd had to read over the weekend.

"How'd *you* do?" she said.

"All right, not great."

"I guess I did okay, too," she said.

"Just okay?"

"Well, you're right. I confess, I aced it."

I smiled. I liked Asa. There was nothing phony about her. "Take a look at these, Silver." Asa passed me a bunch of photos, pictures of the four of them: Jennifer and Asa holding hands. Grant and Patty with their heads together. All of them kicking up their legs.

"We took them at Jen's birthday party," Grant explained.

I didn't say anything. I wondered why she'd asked me to sit with them. I ate my sandwich and listened to them talking.

"And when Wilson Blake came into the court-room and saw my father—" Asa was saying.

"I read about it," Grant broke in. "Didn't he just tell your father what to do? He sounds so arro-gant."

Why was Asa's father in court? Was he the one who was arrogant? No, that didn't make sense. Wilson Blake, then. But who was he? And did I care? What was I even doing here?

"What's your father going to do about that man?" Patty said. She had a bored, sophisticated way of talking, as if she'd heard everything a hundred times before.

"He'll do something, don't worry," Asa said.

"I hope so," Patty said.

"What'd he do?" I asked.

"Blake? For starters, he stole about a million dollars from people who trusted him." Asa sounded excited. Her dark eyes sparkled. "He got them to put their life savings into his company, and then he made terrible, risky investments and lost their money. I think it's the same as stealing outright. Don't you? No better than a thief! And *he* tells my father how to run his courtroom!"

"Your father is a judge?" I asked.

"You don't know Judge Goronkian?" Jennifer gave me a disbelieving look.

The bell rang. Thank goodness! I got up and dumped my milk carton in the wastebasket.

"Sarabeth," Grant called. She caught up with me. "I want to talk to you about the other day when I said you mocked me out." She was talking faster than usual. "I thought about it, and I realized you were trying to stand by me. And I know I didn't act very nice to you."

"No, you didn't."

She blinked. "Do you always say what you're thinking?"

"Sorry. I guess I'm not a very subtle person."

"No, I'm the one who's sorry." We walked down the corridor together. Grant had a little frown between her eyes. "I'm really sorry about the other day, Sarabeth."

She sounded humble. It confused me and at the same time it gave me a kind of confidence with her that I hadn't felt before. I put my hand on her shoulder. "You have character," I said. "That's what my mom says about anybody who does something that's really hard. Like apologizing to another person."

She sighed. "It wasn't that hard." She stopped at the music room, and I kept going. "But it wasn't easy either," she called after me. *"You* didn't make it easy." Then she went into the room.

CHAPTER 13

I was unlocking the door at home when the phone started to ring. I jiggled the key. I had to twist it in a certain way to get it to work, and by the time I got it right, the ringing stopped. Then, a moment later, it started again.

One good thing about living in a trailer, everything is close. I dropped my books on the counter and reached for the phone. At the same moment Tobias got under my feet, and I stepped on his tail. He yowled! I didn't know what to do first, comfort Tobias or pick up the phone, so I tried to do both at once.

"Hello," I said, "hang on, please," and I scooped up Tobias.

"Sarabeth?"

"Yes, it's me."

"This is Mark."

Mark! I hadn't even recognized his voice. It sounded deeper than I remembered, and sort of far away.

"Mark Emelsky," he said. "From the dance—"

"Yes, I know. Wait, Mark. . . . Tobias, don't!" He had put his paws up around my neck and he was hanging there like a huge cat bib.

"Is somebody there?" Mark said. "Maybe this isn't a good time for you?"

"Oh, no, it's only Tobias."

"Who?"

"My cat."

"Oh! I thought maybe it was your brother—or your boyfriend or something."

"I don't have a brother. Or a boyfriend. Just this big lunk of fur." I told him about Tobias's getting under my feet.

"He should meet my cat Paul," Mark said. "Or maybe he shouldn't. Paul is not very bright. When he doesn't want us to see him, he puts his head under a chair and leaves the rest of him sticking out. Maybe he was an ostrich in another life."

I finally unlatched Tobias from my neck and he jumped to the ground. "How much does Paul weigh?" I asked. "Tobias weighs fifteen pounds."

"Paul weighs about six pounds. What do you feed your cat?"

"Cat food. What do you feel Paul, tofu burgers?"

"Sometimes—for supper. Lettuce and eggs with brewer's yeast for breakfast. Don't groan! All three eat it."

"Three? You have three cats?"

"Peter, Paul, and Mary." His voice cracked and went high for a minute. "They're named after the singers from the sixties. My mother thinks that after the Beatles, Peter, Paul, and Mary are the greatest thing on earth, especially Mary. At least once a month, my mother plays this song Mary sings, 'Leavin' on a Jet Plane.' Did you ever hear it?"

"I might have."

"I can quote you every word. When my mother gets in her 'Jet Plane' mood, she plays it over and over until someone screams or throws a fit. . . . What are you doing this weekend?"

"The usual, I guess."

"I'm going to see that space movie at the Fourplex."

"The one about those people from another galaxy who come down to earth and can't figure out what's going on here?"

"Right. They're a thousand times smarter than

we are—in their civilization, everyone has brains like computers—but we have them completely baffled. They can't figure out why we have wars and people go hungry or sleep on streets, stuff like that. For their civilization, it's no problem. It's all simple stuff."

"Do they save the endangered animals in their civilization? Do they have whales there?"

"I hope so! They must have some animals. Are you going to see it?"

"Maybe," I said, but I didn't think so. We didn't go to movies much. They were expensive, and like Mom said, wait long enough and you could catch everything on TV.

"Maybe we could go at the same time," Mark said. "When would you go? Saturday afternoon?"

"No, I'm working on Saturday."

"You have a job? What do you do?"

"I'm a mother's helper."

"What do you help a mother do?"

"Clean up the mess her baby makes."

"Do you have to do that all day?"

"I don't have to do it anytime. Only if I want to."

"Do you want to?"

"Yes. I like making money. . . . My mom was mad when I took the job, though."

"What does she do when she gets mad?"

"She slapped me." I didn't know I was going to tell him that. "Usually, she doesn't do anything but yell," I added quickly.

"When my mom gets mad, she chases me through the house, screaming, 'Mark, when I get my hands on you, you are going to be one sorry kid!' "

"And what does she do?"

"Nothing, because she never catches me. I run faster than she does."

I laughed. Then I told him about Mom working as a housecleaner and how she didn't want me to do the same thing.

"She cleans houses?" he said in his *Huh!* voice. "She probably wants you to do something with more prestige."

"There's nothing wrong with what she does! It's honest work."

"I was just trying to understand your mom's point of view."

"Well . . . you're probably right," I said.

"I am right. I'm right most of the time." Then he said he was going to look for me at the movies on Saturday afternoon. "I'm going to the two o'clock show."

"Look, but you won't see me," I said.

After we hung up, I danced around, shouting, "Mark! Mark! Mark!" How childish! "See you in the Fourplex!" I sang out. I wasn't going. I'd promised to work for Mrs. Vander Burgh. I'd told Mark

I was working, I'd told him I wasn't going—but still I started dreaming about it. My first date. My first almost-date.

I'm getting out of the car in Westwood Mall. A cold, sunny day. The mall is crowded. People hurrying to do their shopping. Sun glinting off cars in the parking lot. A line of kids waiting to go into the movie. Mark waiting for me.

I wave. Hi, Mark!

He smiles (glad to see me). He's wearing his glasses, his braces, and his SAVE THE WHALES T-shirt.

We get in line. What do we talk about? Whales again? Tofu burgers? Boring! Okay, no problem. I start off by telling him that Mom had to work, so Cynthia drove me to the mall.

MARK: *Cynthia sounds nice.*

ME: *I can always count on Cynthia. I call her my second mother.*

MARK: *One mother is enough for me, Sarabeth.*

ME: *Not to change the subject, Mark, but the only thing I don't like about where I live is, no buses.*

MARK: *When you're sixteen, Sarabeth, you can get your driver's license.*

There was a red pillow on the couch. I picked it up and looked at it seriously. "Mark, I'm going to do that," I said.

I leaned back against the couch and put Mark

The Pillow in a reclining position, too. Wait. Weren't we in line for the movie? No, we'd seen the movie already. We'd just come out, and now we were leaning against the wall of the theater, waiting for my mother to pick me up.

"Great movie," I said.

Mark The Pillow stared blankly back at me.

"How about saying something?" I cleared my throat. Mark The Pillow cleared his throat.

"That's a beginning," I said encouragingly.

"That's a beginning," Mark The Pillow said.

"I'm sure you can do better than that," I said.

Mark The Pillow had that blank look on his face.

"Try," I said.

"Try," Mark The Pillow said.

"I wish I was sixteen already," I said.

"I wish I was sixteen already," he said.

"Congratulations on a long sentence!" I pounded him on his back. "Why do you wish you were sixteen?"

"I'd rather be a grown-up than a kid," Mark The Pillow said.

"I know what you mean. Sometimes it's quite irritating being our age." I told him how much I longed to hear Cynthia sing professionally. "I'll probably have to wait until I'm eighteen."

Mark The Pillow thought that was too bad. He agreed with me that my mother was over-protective.

"You know," I said, "your face looks a little blank today. I don't mean to hurt your feelings. It's not your fault." I hurried down the hall to my room. I found a black felt-tipped pen and gave Mark The Pillow a pair of large, wide-open eyes. "That's better, isn't it?" I asked.

Mark The Pillow agreed in his deep, manly voice. "I feel much more lively and awake now, Sarabeth. But I think I need glasses to really see well."

"Oops, I forgot! Sorry about that." I gave him glasses.

"Thank you," he said. "You're very sweet."

I liked the way he looked at me with his wide-open eyes. "I want to kiss you," he said.

"Mark! You can't do it. You don't have a mouth."

"Well, give me one," he said. "Quick! I can't wait!"

I took the felt-tip and gave him a smiling mouth with teeth and braces. Right away, he kissed me. Then he pulled back and looked at me. "Did you like that?"

"Yes," I said. My face was burning.

Mark The Pillow bobbed his head and came close to me again. "Sarabeth. *You* could kiss *me.*"

Another great idea! Why hadn't I thought of it? I pressed my lips to his. "You have such soft lips," I said.

Mark The Pillow smiled at me, showing his braces. Lucky me! I hadn't even felt them when I kissed him.

"You know, Mark, if Mom saw me doing this, she'd have a fit. Alone in the house and kissing!"

"You think she'd get mad again?" he said.

"Oh, she might. It depends on her mood."

"My mother chases me through the house when she gets mad. She yells, 'Mark, when I get my hands on you . . .' "

"And then what?" I asked.

"Then, nothing," Mark The Pillow said. "I run faster than she does."

"Oh, you darling, adorable boy!" I kissed him passionately, again and again.

"Sarabeth? Sarabeth, what are you doing?"

I looked up. My mother was standing in the doorway, staring at me.

I dropped the pillow face down. "Sorry, Mark," I mumbled.

"What's going on, Sarabeth?" Mom said. "You look so funny. Your face is all blotchy. Are you getting sick? Are you feverish?"

"I'm fine." I shoved Mark The Pillow behind me. "Mom," I said in a firm voice, "we have to do something with that front-door lock. I almost didn't get it open today."

"I noticed it was getting worse. I have to tighten the screws on the plate. Get me the screwdriver, hon, I'll do it right now."

She walked into the kitchen. I got the screwdriver from our toolbox under the bathroom sink. Later, I rescued Mark The Pillow from the couch and put him in my closet.

CHAPTER 14

Saturday morning, Mom said, "I want you to go grocery shopping with me later this afternoon."

I poured milk into my cornflakes. "When?"

"I'll be back from work around four or four-thirty."

Just the time when Mark and I would have come out of the movies. I stood up to get the sugar bowl. "Okay, I'm working for Mrs. Vander Burgh until four."

Mom frowned. She still didn't like that I was doing housework. "Those jeans are getting too tight for you, Sarabeth. Maybe I'll buy you a pair later."

They were my favorite jeans. Calvin Klein. Mom had found them for a dollar at a rummage sale in the Episcopal church. I had to hold my breath when I zipped them up, but I didn't care. "I can buy myself new jeans, Mom. I'll have enough money after today. No, I'll give you the money and you can pay back Cynthia some more."

"Sarabeth, I take care of that. Don't worry about it."

"Please don't say that! 'Don't worry about it, don't worry about it.' You say that all the time."

Mom clattered her plate into the sink. "What is this? I can't say anything around here anymore."

"Oh, huff, huff."

She gave me a glance over her shoulder. " 'Huff, huff'? What does that mean?"

"I don't know, it just jumped into my mind."

"Well, jump it out. It sounds fresh to me."

"*Ooog!*" I said.

"*Ooog? Ooog!* What's going on, Sarabeth? Are you trying to make me crazy?"

I pulled a paper bag over my head. "Sorry, lady," I said from inside the bag, "I can't tell you the answer to that question. I'm a victim of my weird mind." I lifted the bag a little so I could see out. Mom was pinching her mouth the way she does when she doesn't want to laugh at something silly or stupid I've done.

The supermarket Mom likes is out on Cathay Road. It's huge, and it's always jammed on Saturdays. You can hardly push through the people and carts in the aisles, and the lines at the checkout counters are really long. Mom and I had been standing in line for about ten minutes when I saw Grant at the customer-service desk. She was wearing a black jacket and white sneakers, and she had her hair done in about six braids.

"Look at that headline," Mom said. She pointed to a newspaper in the rack in front of the checkout counter. SIX-YEAR-OLD GIRL COMES BACK FROM THE DEAD. TELLS TALES OF HORROR. SHE WAS ON THE OTHER SIDE! "Isn't that amazing?"

"Mom, you don't believe that stuff."

Mom shrugged. She looked embarrassed. "I guess not, but it would be fascinating if somebody really did come back from the dead." She picked up the newspaper and started to read the story.

Grant was walking toward us.

"Mom, don't buy that," I whispered. "Don't waste our money."

"Sarabeth, I'm just looking at it."

"Put it back!"

Grant got in our line. I wasn't sure if she'd seen me or not.

"Mom," I said between my teeth.

"Shh, Sarabeth! I've got to do something to keep from going crazy while we wait."

"Sarabeth!" Grant had noticed me.

I turned around as if I'd just seen her. "Oh, hi."

She came up past the other people and stood in line with me. She was carrying a quart of milk and a bag of roasted peanuts. "Hi, what're you doing here?" she said. "I mean, isn't this pretty far out from where you live?"

"My mother likes shopping here," I said. Mom glanced up from her newspaper, and I introduced Grant.

"You go to the same school?" Mom said.

I could see her eyes lighting up. I could see the words *Best Friend* lighting up her mind. Forget it, Mom, I thought.

"I like your shirt, Sarabeth," Grant said. Over a turtleneck I was wearing an old shirt of Billy's tied at the waist.

"Great braids," I said.

The man behind us was listening. "Young girls like to talk to each other," he said.

He was a little man with silver-gray hair. He wore his coat buttoned up to his chin, as if he were freezing. He had two overflowing shopping baskets, one in front of him and one behind him. "I'm shopping for a large family. But not my family. My neighbor's family. What do you think of that?"

Grant and I glanced at each other. "That's very nice of you," I said.

"Well, my neighbor is somewhat incapacitated," he said. "I can help her out a little, so I do. I'm still driving, you see, and I have no one but myself. So does it hurt me to do her shopping?"

He paused, as if waiting for an answer.

We looked at each other again. "I guess not," Grant said.

"You are right. It does not hurt me. In fact, I can tell you this truthfully, it gives me a real pleasure to help another human being." He smiled shyly at us. "Talk, young girls," he said. "Don't mind me. Talk to each other. Go ahead." And he waved his hands over us, as if he were blessing us.

CHAPTER 15

Monday morning Grant sat down on my desk. "That little man was so funny," she said. "And sweet."

"Yes, but I kept wanting to giggle."

"Oh, Sarabeth!"

"Come on, you wanted to laugh, too," I said. "You did! Admit it. Snort, snort! Giggle, giggle!"

"Snort, snort, giggle, giggle?"

"Right! Snort, snort, giggle, giggle."

Later Grant caught up to me in the hall and said, in a fast whisper, "Snort snort giggle giggle." Then, all week, whenever we saw each other, one or the other of us would say the four awful words like a secret password.

Mark called me. "Hi," he said.

"Hi! I was thinking about calling you."

"Why didn't you?"

"Because you called first," I said.

"I'll hang up."

"No!"

"Yes. Goodbyyyye. . . ."

"Mark!"

A click. Then silence.

I dialed his number.

"Hello?" he said.

"Hello."

"Sarabeth! Hey, how are you? Long time no hear."

"At least six seconds."

"I thought it was more like ten."

A good beginning, but then neither of us said anything. And then both of us started to talk at the same time.

"You go first," I said.

"No, you," he said.

"How was the movie?"

"What movie?"

"The movie."

"The movie?" he repeated.

"The one about the beings from another planet."

"Oh, that one. I didn't go."

"You didn't *go?* You didn't see it on Saturday?"

"No, I decided to watch my sister play basketball instead."

"I thought she played tennis."

"That's Shana. Kate plays basketball."

"Is she good?"

"Not really. She's okay. She gets all excited about the games."

"I still can't believe you didn't go to the movie."

"What's so hard about believing that?"

"Well . . . what if *I'd* gone? I mean, you said you'd look for me there."

Mark didn't say anything. I felt suddenly so upset, just as if I *had* gone to the movies—looking for him, expecting to see him, and not finding him.

"Did you go?" he said, finally.

"No. I was working."

"So, I don't understand."

"Well, what if I had decided not to work and gone to the movies instead? You *said* you'd be there."

"I changed my mind. Don't you ever change your mind?"

"Yes."

"Okay then."

"Okay," I said. I didn't know what I was saying okay to. We talked for a couple more minutes, then we hung up.

*   *   *

Thursday, Grant waved me over to her table in the cafeteria. As soon as I sat down, she said, "Snort snort giggle giggle."

"What's that?" Asa asked.

"A joke of Silver's and mine."

"Sounds really funny," Jennifer muttered.

Patty gave me a bored, owlish stare.

The next day, Grant and I agreed we'd worn the joke out. "Just have to get another one," I said.

"Goodbye, snort snort giggle giggle." Grant put her arm through mine.

I glanced down at our linked arms. *We're friends,* I thought. *We're really friends.*

CHAPTER 16

"Why didn't you sit with us at lunch today?" Grant said, catching up with me in the hall. "Didn't you see me waving to you?"

"I had homework to do," I said.

I had been eating lunch with Grant and the other three quite often, but sometimes I went off and sat down by myself. I could take only so much of Patty, Jennifer, and Asa. They weren't what I would call exactly friendly toward me. Asa was the friendliest, Patty the coolest. She always gave me that aloof face, like a shiny penny, bright, almost blank. Jennifer was somewhere in between, not really welcoming, but not completely distant either.

"I don't think Patty and the others are too thrilled about me horning in on you guys," I said.

Grant frowned. "Sarabeth, you are not horning in. This tight little clique stuff gets on my nerves. There're more people in the world than just us four. We're always with each other. It's getting boring! Sit with us tomorrow," she ordered.

The way she said that made me smile. Grant could be a little queenly now and then.

I went home with her that day after school. Mom had said she'd pick me up when she was done working. We walked to Grant's house, uphill all the way. Bridwell Lane, where she lived, was one enormous house after another. The chimneys were huge, the lawns gigantic. The garages could have swallowed up two, three, or even four Roadview trailers. Every house had a three- or four-car garage. And parked in every driveway was either a very, very big car or a very, very small car.

There was one of each in Grant's driveway. The small car, a green MG, was her stepfather's. "It's his play car," she said. "He drives a BMW to work." The big car, a black Mercedes, was her mother's "play car." "She drives a Honda to work," Grant said.

I nodded, as if every family I knew had four cars.

We went into the house. "Sadie?" Grant called. "Oh, I guess she's not here," she said.

"Your mother?"

"No, the housekeeper."

I nodded again.

My first impression of her house was of a tremendous amount of space and light. The ceilings were high, the walls were all a creamy light color, and the floors were covered with thick, smoky-green carpeting. I saw the living room on one side and the dining room on the other. Big couches, chairs and tables everywhere. I kept blinking my eyes—I don't know why. It was like being in a store, everything new and beautiful. I felt I should tiptoe and speak in a hushed voice.

"Need the bathroom?" Grant said.

I shook my head.

"I'm floating." She went off to the bathroom.

I looked around, wondering if Mom worked in any houses like this. There was a crystal chandelier in the dining room that looked like something out of a movie. In the center of the room was a long, dark, shiny table with a big bowl of real flowers in the middle and twelve chairs around it.

A stone fireplace in the living room was tall enough to walk into. There was a grand piano in one corner of the room, shining like everything else, and little bowls of candy everywhere. I tiptoed over to a table and took a candy wrapped in gold paper. I folded the gold paper and put it into my pocket. The candy was delicious, it tasted of raspberry and chocolate mixed together.

Grant came back and I slid the candy guiltily

into the side of my cheek. "Come on, let's get something to eat," she said.

The kitchen was bigger than the dining room. It ran the whole width of the back of the house. Copper pots and wire baskets hung from hooks in the ceiling, and there was a brick fireplace in the middle of the room and two of everything: two sinks, two stoves, two refrigerators, two freezers, even two toasters and two blenders.

"Peanut butter sandwiches and milkshakes sound okay to you?" Grant asked.

"Fine." It was the same thing I would have made if we'd gone to my house. *Gone to my house?* How could I ever bring Grant to my house? She'd walk into the kitchen and think she was in a closet. She'd go into the living room and think it was where we stored our old furniture.

Grant opened one of the refrigerators. I peered over her shoulder. I'd never seen so much food in one place outside a supermarket. The shelves were stuffed with everything you could think of. She took out a carton of milk and a bottle of strawberry flavoring and handed them to me.

She opened a covered dish. A white, slimy mold covered the top of something that looked vaguely like meat. "That Sadie," Grant said. "She's always letting things go bad." She dumped the mess into the sink and turned on the disposal unit.

We made the shakes and sandwiches, working

at the butcher-block counter. "How do you decide which one?" I said.

"Which one what?"

"The refrigerators. How do you choose?"

Grant looked blank for a moment, then she said, "Oh, I see what you're asking. Well that one"—she pointed to the avocado-colored refrigerator—"is just for parties and things. This one over here is for our regular everyday food. The same with the freezers. Let's go up to my room, okay?" She got straws and napkins and put everything on a tray. "Want anything else?"

I shook my head.

She looked at me closely. "Are you all right, Sarabeth?"

I nodded.

"You've hardly said two words since we came in. Are you sure you're okay?"

"Yeah—I mean, *yes.*"

Grant kept looking at me with that little frown between her eyes. "I don't know," she said. "You don't seem like yourself."

"No, I'm fine. Let's go." I took the tray.

Even the stairs impressed me. They were broad and carpeted. The curved mahogany banister gleamed with polish and wax. I went up ahead of Grant, holding the tray carefully. I'd die if I spilled anything in this perfect house.

Grant had fallen behind me. Suddenly she raced

up to me and shouted in my ear, "Snort snort giggle giggle!"

I jumped, the tray tipped, the glasses rattled. "You idiot, Grant, I almost dropped everything!"

Grant looked pleased. "Drop it!" She tried to grab the tray from me. I twisted away. She got her arms around me and jiggled the tray. "Drop it! Drop it, Sarabeth."

"Stop!" I dumped the tray into her hands. "If you want to drop it, go ahead."

She laughed and we went on up the stairs. Halfway up, where they turned, there was a little landing with a stained-glass window over a padded window seat. "I bet this is your favorite place." I imagined curling up, reading, Tobias in my lap.

"Definitely not," Grant said. "Too public."

In the upstairs hall, I peeked into a bathroom. Carpeting, two sinks, a shower with glass doors, a huge round tub sunk into the floor, gold faucets.

Grant's room wasn't as overwhelming as the rest of the house, although it was large and everything matched perfectly. She had a walk-in closet filled with clothes. I especially liked her bed with the flowered canopy. "I'd give it to you if I could," she said, putting down the tray. "It's not my taste. My mother and Evan picked it out when they got married and bought this house."

"When was that?" We sat on the floor and drank our shakes.

"Three—no, four years ago. Evan bought everything new."

"Do you like him?"

"He's all right. He's generous, he can be funny—tells funny stories, has a good sense of humor. Sometimes we don't get along, though. He's sort of domineering. He always wants me to have what he likes and do what he wants. He wants me to call him Dad, that's one of the things we fight about."

"I can't imagine you fighting," I said.

"Well, it's not a real fight, just a long-term argument." She put a piece of sheet music on a music stand. "I'm going to play something for you." She took her flute out of its case. "This flute is one great thing Evan bought me." She lifted it to her lips. "Tell me if you like this."

I sat on the rug, listening. The music made me think of water and flowers and springtime.

"Well?" she said when she was done.

"I liked it. It was pretty. . . . It made me think of flowers." I was embarrassed and looked into the bottom of my glass. What if that was a foolish thing to say?

"Flowers? Honestly? Great." For Grant, that was enthusiasm. "I wrote it," she said.

"You composed that yourself? I'm impressed. That's talent."

"Do you think so?" She looked anxious. "I wish I knew if I was really talented."

We lay across her bed and talked. She told me that before her mother married Evan, she had been a surgical nurse. "After they got married, he didn't want her to do that anymore. He said it paid just about enough to buy bird food. He wanted her to work with him in his business. So she does. She's the office manager, she does all the ordering."

Grant took an album down from her bookshelf to show me pictures of her family. "This is my sister, Missie, Sarabeth."

"She's beautiful."

"She's so great, Sarabeth. You have to meet her sometime. She's in medical school."

"My mother would like me to be a doctor."

"Are you going to?"

"No, I'd rather be a famous chef."

"That's original." She turned the page. "Look, Sarabeth, here's my mom."

I expected Grant's mother to look like her and her sister, blonde and serene. But she was dark-haired, plumpish, and had a little worried smile on her face. It was Grant's stepfather, though, who really surprised me. He was a tall, fat man, with small blurred features. He was wearing sneakers and a stretched-out T-shirt.

"I didn't think he'd look like that," I said. Grant glanced at me. My face went hot. How embarrassing it would be to have to explain that I had assumed because they were rich, her parents would be sleek and beautiful.

We started talking about our fathers. Grant said the last time she heard anything about her father was eight years ago, when a friend of her mother's saw her father in San Diego. "When my sister went to Reed College in Oregon, she said she was going to try to find our father. One vacation she did go to San Diego, but"—Grant shrugged—"she couldn't find out anything."

"You never hear from him?"

"Never," she said.

"Sometimes I imagine my father isn't really dead and he's going to call me up and say, 'I wasn't killed in that accident. I had amnesia all this time.'" I stopped. I didn't really believe that, not anymore. It was something I used to think about when I was younger.

"If my father called on the phone," Grant said, and her voice flattened out, "I'd hang up on him. If he showed up at our house, I'd slam the door in his face." She put the album away and sat down in front of her dressing table. "My father left us when I was a baby. Missie was seven years old. I wish he had died."

"No you don't," I said.

She turned around, holding a little gray tube of mascara. "Yes I do, Sarabeth! *Your* father died, and that's sad, but you can *be* sad about it. You're lucky, Sarabeth. I think it's better to be sad than to feel the way I do.'' She leaned forward and quickly brushed mascara onto her eyelashes. Her cheeks were mottled. She kept putting on makeup—lip gloss, eyeliner, a whole bunch of stuff. And then she wiped it all off, and after a while she was calm again.

I guess you don't really know a person until you talk to them alone. Grant was different that afternoon, different from the way I'd seen her in school, different from when we were with the other girls. She was more intense, she was sadder, and she was freer, too, in some ways. Maybe I was different, too.

When I heard a car horn outside, I went to the window. It was Mom. She had parked our old rust bucket right behind Evan's gorgeous little MG. Maybe she was sitting there dreaming about having a little green sports car like that! ''Mom!'' I rapped on the window and waved.

Grant and I went downstairs together. ''Thanks for asking me over,'' I said.

''You have to come again, Silver. You know what? I think I'll always call you Silver from now on. It suits you. Your eyes are sort of silvery. They're beautiful.''

''They are?'' Nobody had ever told me that.

''Oh, I almost forgot! I knew there was something I was going to tell you. Saturday night we're having a pajama party. Will you come?"

"Ohhh, wait, let me think if I can," I said, as if I had a dozen things claiming my attention. I'd been hoping that Mrs. Vander Burgh would ask me to baby-sit for Geri, but there was nothing set.

"It's our first pajama party of the season," Grant said. "Every year, the four of us each have one. We eat supper, we sleep over, and we have breakfast together the next morning. We always start with Patty and revolve around."

"It's at Patty's house?" I said. We were in the hall. "I can't go there, Grant, she didn't invite me."

"I'm inviting you," Grant said. "It's okay. Say you'll come, Silver." She put her hands on my shoulders and looked into my face.

I thought how, only a week ago, if someone had told me I'd be in Grant's house, listening to her half order, half beg me to come to a pajama party, I wouldn't have believed it.

CHAPTER 17

Friday, I was in the locker room getting ready for gym, when Patty sat down on the bench next to me. She'd had gym the period before, and she'd just come out of the shower and was drying her hair. "Hi, Sarabeth," she said in her cool, listless voice.

"Hi, Patty."

"Ready for volleyball?" she asked. "Mr. Cooper's on his volleyball kick."

I knew she hadn't come over to give me that news. Suddenly I thought, *She's going to tell me not to come to the pajama party.* My face flushed. She was going to humiliate me. What should I say? *That's fine with me, Patty. I didn't want to come in the first place . . . only Grant begged me. . . . Actually, Patty, your timing is perfect, I was about to tell you I have something better to do.*

"The funniest thing happened yesterday," she said. "I was at a party, and I met a boy I used to know in grade school." She glanced over at me. "Mark Emelsky. He said he knew you."

"Really." I tried to sound as cool and bored as she did. I put my foot up on the bench and tied my laces.

"He said the two of you were friends."

"Really?" I heard myself doing a Frankie Klematis.

"Good friends." Patty tested a strand of hair, then toweled it some more.

"He said you were a pretty great person."

I couldn't even say *really!* I was struck dumb that Mark would say that about me. And that Patty would repeat it was so generous. It was like giving me a present!

Jennifer came up behind us. "Did I hear someone say Mark Emelsky's name? I know him."

"We all know him," Patty said. The bell rang, and she gathered up her books and her hairbrush.

Jennifer and I went up the stairs to the gym. "Where'd you meet Mark?" she asked.

"At the school dance."

"What was he doing at our dance? I thought he went to Persian."

"He does, he just came over."

"To see you?"

"No, we didn't know each other until the dance.

I was alone and he was alone, so we started to talk."

In the gym, Jennifer picked up a basketball. "One on one," she said. I put my arms out, blocking her. She made a basket. I got the ball and threw it. It bounced off the rim.

"Go up higher," Jennifer said. She leaped and made another basket. "He was always sort of a weird kid."

"Who, Mark?"

"Yeah, strange type."

"No, he's really nice," I said, annoyed.

Jennifer looked at me. "I didn't say he wasn't."

Mr. Cooper came in and called everybody to order. "Line up and count off."

We played volleyball all period. Jennifer and I ended up on the same team. She was the star player, all over the court, always breaking out of her position, but nobody got too mad because she made so many great saves. Even up at the net, short as she was, she could go up in the air and spike.

Halfway through the period, Mr. Cooper called a break. We sat down against the wall. "I *love* volleyball," Jennifer said. "It's so much fun! Don't you think so?"

"It's okay. I'm not very good at it."

"You could be better, Sarabeth. Keep your forearms stiffer and bend your knees more."

I went back down into the locker room for a

drink. Jennifer was behind me. "Mark must be growing up, if you like him," she said, taking a gulp of water. "He was the shy type when we went to grade school together."

"He still is, somewhat." I thought of Mark The Pillow. And then I heard myself saying, "He kissed me." I heard the words coming out of my mouth, and my face started burning.

"He kissed you?" Jennifer repeated.

"Well . . . well . . ." I stammered.

"Oh, look at you, all red! What was this, your first kiss?"

"I guess so, yes."

"Your first kiss!" Her hair seemed to stand out all around her head with excitement. "Wild!"

"I shouldn't have told you that, Jennifer. I shouldn't have said it."

"Why not?"

"It's, it's—a secret. Mark asked me not to tell anybody," I improvised.

"I *looove* secrets."

"Jennifer, you won't repeat it?"

"Me?" She got a silly, sly look on her face.

She's going to tell someone, I thought. Even if she isn't planning to, it's going to come out.

"Mark," she said. "Little old Mark Emelsky. Is he a good kisser?" She gave me another sly look.

"It wasn't actually a real kiss," I said.

"What do you mean, not a *real* kiss? It wasn't on the mouth, or what? Where was it, then?"

"It was—you know, everywhere."

"Everywhere!" She shook her hand in that gesture that meant, *Whew!* "If that isn't real, I don't know what is. . . . And you seem such a quiet type, Sarabeth."

"Jennifer, I didn't mean it that way. Not *everywhere.* Just—here, cheeks and—" I was totally rattled and patted myself all over my face. I should have said, *No, no, no, no!* I should have told the truth and stopped the whole thing. *No, Jennifer! No, not Mark Emelsky. Mark The Pillow. I was kissed by a pillow, Jennifer.*

Grant met me outside the cafeteria. "Silver, I was waiting for you." She linked arms with me. "I brought my lunch today." Usually she bought something at the hot table. "I thought we could share. I have cream cheese and walnuts. What do you have?"

"Bologna and cheese."

"I love bologna, and my mother will never buy it."

We sat down. The others were already there. I'd just opened my lunch bag when Jennifer said, "Listen, everyone! Guess what? Sarabeth had her first kiss."

"Jennifer!" I dropped my sandwich. "You said you wouldn't tell!"

"I won't! You didn't mean *us,* did you?"

"Who was it?" Asa asked. "Who kissed you?"

"You'll never guess," Jennifer said. "Guess!"

"Mark Emelsky," Patty said in her weariest voice, but I saw a little smile in the corners of her mouth.

"How'd you know that?" Jennifer demanded.

"Mark Emelsky?" Asa said. "Mark the Mouthpiece?"

"The very one," Jennifer said. She pushed out her upper lip with her tongue, so it looked as if she had buck teeth. They all burst out laughing.

"He has braces now," I said. Why did I say anything? They all knew him from grade school, and they had plenty to say.

Grant slapped her forehead. "That was *Mark* you were dancing with, wasn't it?" She passed me half of her sandwich. "Mark Emelsky! I can't believe it. I looked right at him and I didn't know it was him. I remember thinking he looked vaguely familiar."

"So he's the vegetarian you told us about," Asa said, rolling her big brown eyes. "Now that makes sense. Mark always had a cause. When the rest of us got up there with pinwheels and stuffed animals for Show and Tell, Mark unrolled a poster of endangered wild flowers."

"Remember the time in third grade when he brought that filthy cat into class?" Patty said.

"And wanted us to adopt it as our class mascot?" Asa laughed. "I always liked Mark."

"Mark, the animal saint. He found that cat in the gutter, and it was in bad shape. Oh, it stunk." Jennifer held her nose. "Mr. Luft made him take it out."

"He probably brought it home as a present for his mom," Grant said.

They all laughed again and started clamoring to hear about the kiss. "Oh, Sarabeth, first kiss!" Asa had a little trill in her voice. "Tell us what it was like."

"Nothing," I said. "Really, nothing."

"It was not 'nothing,' " Jennifer said. "Don't believe her! He kissed her all over."

"All over?" Asa repeated.

Patty stared at me. Did she guess that I wasn't telling the truth?

"It wasn't like that," I said. "It was just . . . Nobody tell Mark that I said it. *Please.* I don't want to hurt his feelings," I added. Which made about as much sense as when I said Mark wanted me to keep our "kiss" a secret.

"His *feelings,*" Jennifer said. "Guys don't get their feelings hurt when they talk about kissing and sex, Sarabeth. They just boast and get puffed up, don't you know that?"

I looked into my lunch bag, wishing I could dive

straight into it. What if one of them told Mark I'd said all these things? Somebody was sure to tell him! *Sarabeth Silver says you kissed her. She says you kissed her all over!* He wouldn't think I was such a great person, then. He'd think I was a liar, an idiot, and a total flake.

Asa pushed her glasses up on her nose. "What kind of kisses were they? Passionate?"

"No, Asa."

"Gentle?"

"Asa!"

"Loud, enthusiastic smackers?"

"Can we please talk about something else?"

"Sure." Jennifer leaned toward me. "Did he grapple you?"

I rolled my eyes. "I refuse to say anything else. The subject is closed." Then I made the mistake of thinking about Mark The Pillow, and I snickered.

That was all Jennifer needed. She almost bounced out of her seat. "He grappled you!"

"He didn't, I didn't say that."

"Too bad he didn't kiss you on the mouth," Asa said, "though I'd settle for a cheek kiss, myself. I haven't even had that yet."

"I got kissed for the first time in fourth grade," Jennifer said.

"Yes, Jennifer," Asa said, "we know all about it."

"By the time I was in sixth grade—"

"Yes, Jennifer," Asa and Grant chorused together.

"I do something different every year," Jennifer went on, ignoring them.

"Yes, Jennifer, we've heard all about it."

"Oh, you two," Jennifer said. "You especially, Grant. You don't care if you aren't kissed until you're sixteen."

"Seventeen," Grant said.

"Seven*teen*," Jennifer moaned. "That's *old.*"

"Jennifer, you're going to be old before your time."

"Sex is part of life," Jennifer said. "As long as you don't do anything stupid—"

"Yes, Jennifer," Asa and Grant and Patty all said together, and I joined in. "Yes, Jennifer, we've heard all about it!"

I was laughing. For the first time, I felt part of the group. I turned to Patty. "What about you?"

"What about me?"

"Have you been kissed?"

"What do you think?"

"I think, yes. Must be."

"Oh, really?" She said coolly.

"Yes, I think you're beautiful."

"*Ooooh,*" Jennifer sang out, "Sarabeth has a crush on Patty."

That embarrassed me and, trying to cover up, I made things worse. I held up my fist like a microphone and said, "Will the beautiful Ms. Lewis answer a few questions for her many fans? Ms. Lewis, tell us about your experience with—"

"Shut up." Patty's eyes went flat, hostile. "You don't know what you're talking about."

I stared at her with a stupid, leftover smile.

Patty pushed away from the table and went out.

"Uh-oh," Asa said. "Pattycake just got into a mood." Then they all started talking about something else. Patty didn't come back.

CHAPTER 18

"Did I tell you where Patty lives?" Grant asked.

I shifted the phone to my other ear. "Yeah, you did."

"Not yeah, *yes,*" Mom said in the background. She and Leo were making supper and listening to everything I said.

"I don't think I'm going to the pajama party, Grant."

"Oh, Silver, why?"

"Sarabeth!" Mom said behind me.

I waved Mom away. "Grant, you were there yesterday. You heard Patty. And did you see the look she gave me?"

"Patty has moods," Grant said. "And she always comes out of them. We're all used to them.

You'll see, Silver, tonight she'll be fine."

I finally let Grant persuade me, partly because Mom was having a fit. "She's more excited about the party than you are," Leo said to me. All the way over to Patty's house on Shadow Lane Road, Mom kept asking me if I'd forgotten anything. "Did you take your toothbrush? Hairbrush? Slippers?"

"Jane, let up," Leo said. "Sarabeth's only going for overnight." I patted his shoulder. "Anytime, pal," he said.

Patty lived in a yellow house with black shutters—not as big as I expected, but not small either. Grant was waiting for me outside. I drew in a big breath, kissed Mom, and got out of the car.

Grant took me around the side of Patty's house. We went in through the garage to the kitchen. I heard voices from the front of the house. "Hi, Mrs. Lewis," Grant called. "It's Grant and Sarabeth Silver."

"Hello, Grant," a man's voice called.

Grant smiled. "Hello, Mr. Dexter. . . . That's Patty's uncle," she said to me.

We went upstairs to the second floor.

Patty's room was the last one at the end of the hall. Jennifer and Asa were already there. Asa was bent over, plugging a popcorn machine into a wall socket, and Jennifer was unrolling a bunch of blue foam camp mattresses.

"Hi, Sarabeth," Patty said. She looked beautiful and glamorous in loose turquoise pants and top and round silver earrings. "I'm really glad you came." She looked right into my eyes and she reached out and half hugged me. It surprised me and made me feel good. I stopped being angry about the day before.

I looked around. There were deep red drapes on the windows and the floor was covered with a woven blue and red rug. The aura in the room was strong, intense. Behind Patty's desk, every inch of the wall was covered with pictures of faraway places—snow-topped mountains and little streets with small white houses.

I threw down my knapsack. "Patty, I love your room. . . . Can I do anything?"

"Yes! Help me with these stupid mattresses. They keep rolling back up on me," Jennifer said.

We flattened the mattresses and piled them on top of each other under the window. Jennifer flung herself down full-length on them and stared at her fingernails. "I have to stop biting my nails," she said to no one in particular.

Asa had the popcorn machine going. "It's heating up," she yelled over the noise of the motor.

Patty and Grant were looking at some clothes in Patty's closet. I sat down next to Jennifer. That was when I saw the door wall. For me, it was exactly like the first time I saw the Goldmobile. For a moment I didn't know what I was looking at—and then, when I understood, I didn't want to stop looking.

The entire wall was a painting. There were three "layers" to the painting. Near the ceiling, a girl with her hands crossed on her chest floated in a blue sky. She looked calm, dreamy. In a way, it reminded me of the picture of my family that I'd made in first grade, with my father as a water bug. He'd been floating in the sky, too, but that was where the resemblance ended. This was superior to anything I'd ever done or could hope to do. And it was the only peaceful, happy part of the painting.

Below the floating girl was the second "layer" of the painting, a falling girl—falling through the middle of the wall, her hair streaming out, her mouth open in fear.

Below her, crossing the door, was still another figure—and now I realized that all three figures were the same girl. The third girl was running— running to something or away from something.

I got up and opened the door. The running girl split in half: she seemed to be running out of one side of the picture and tumbling into the other side.

"Patty did that," Asa said proudly.

"I didn't know you were an artist, Patty."

"I'm not," Patty said, turning around. "I just did that because I felt like it."

"You could be an artist," Grant said. "You have the talent. If you wanted to, you could win all the art prizes, Patty."

Patty tossed her hair impatiently. You could tell she didn't want to talk about it. "Okay, we're all here, let's officially start our pajama party." She took a tall green bottle off her bureau. "Champagne, anybody?"

I hadn't noticed the five wine glasses lined up on the bureau. My heart thumped. I knew the way Mom felt about alcohol. Patty poured the champagne and passed around the glasses.

Asa raised her glass. "My dear friends," she began in a deep voice, "tonight we are gathered here to—"

"Someone stop Judge Asa, *please*," Jennifer said.

"Silence," Asa said. "My toast is to all the fun and pajama parties we're going to have this year."

"Okay, I'm for that."

"Jennifer, I'm not done. Restrain yourself. And my toast is to us five friends."

Grant clinked her glass against mine. *Five friends?* Asa winked at me. I looked at Patty and Jennifer. They weren't clinking or winking. Well, maybe *three* friends. I dipped my tongue into the champagne. It was bubbly, a sandy reddish color. It tasted sweet and tingly. Bubbles went up my nose.

It was so good I felt I could drink it right down, and that scared me. Wasn't alcohol supposed to be an acquired taste? I made myself take tiny sips.

"Don't you like it?" Jennifer asked. Everyone was finished except me. "You don't have to be polite, Sarabeth. If you don't want it, I'll take your share. I love this stuff."

"Leave her drink alone, piggy. You can have more of your own," Asa said. She passed around a big bowl of buttered popcorn and turned on the machine again.

I drank the next two glasses a little faster, all the while staring at Patty's wall painting. Floating girl, falling girl, running girl. Floating girl . . . falling girl . . . running girl. . . . The longer I stared, the dizzier I felt.

My glass was empty again. Was I drinking too much? Getting high? Was I going to make a fool of myself in front of everyone?

Suddenly Asa screamed. Popcorn was flowing over the top of the bowl, bouncing over the floor.

"Popcorn escapees!" I cried. Patty laughed. I liked that, it incited me to more silliness. "Quick! Round them up! Where's the lasso?" I jumped up, slipped, and sat down hard on my butt. That's what happens when you drink, I thought. First you're dizzy, then you're silly, then you get stupid, and then there's an accident.

"No more champagne," I said. "I'm too high."

"You're what?" Asa said.

"Hiiiiigh," I said, lifting my arm high above my head. "High, high, *high."*

They were all looking at me and laughing. "She's high."

"Oh, yeah, hi," Jennifer said, waving her hand.

"Tsk, tsk," Asa said.

Grant took pity on me. "Silver, it's not the real stuff." She handed me the green bottle. It had a red label that said: APPLE SHANGPAIGN. ALCOHOL-FREE.

"Shangpaign?" I said.

"Fizzy apple juice," Jennifer said. "We always have it at our parties, fool!"

CHAPTER 19

The door to Patty's room swung open. "Don't come in, damn it!" Patty yelled. Her face went red.

"It's me, Patty."

"Oh, Mom." Patty put her chin in her hands.

Patty's mother was carrying a big cardboard box. "Supper," she said, *"and* a photo opportunity." She had a camera strung around her neck. Mrs. Lewis looked like a grown-up Patty—same blonde hair, same full red lips. She was wearing jeans and a soft green flannel shirt. She had very pale skin, and I noticed her hands especially—they were white and soft with long pink nails.

I stared at her and I thought, *That's the kind of woman who has my mother in to clean her house while she goes to the beauty parlor for a manicure.*

My mother never had long nails—she kept them clipped short for work—and the skin on her hands was sort of brownish and dry, with veins and lines across the backs.

Mrs. Lewis put down the cardboard box. "Hi, Grant! Hi, Jenny sweetie. Oh, Asa, how are you?" She had a word for everyone. She looked at me. "You're Sarabeth? Welcome, Sarabeth. It's truly nice to see a new face here." She shook my hand and sort of squeezed it. "Are you all ready to have your pictures taken?" she said.

Asa groaned. "Leave me out, I take a terrible picture."

"Asa, stop that whining. It's our tradition," Grant said. "Silver, come stand next to me."

We lined up with our arms around each other. I was between Grant and Jennifer. Jennifer dropped her hand on my shoulder like a stone.

The camera was a Polaroid, and Mrs. Lewis took enough shots so we each had a picture. "Asa," Grant said, studying her picture, "why do you always roll your eyes up into your head that way?"

Asa took Grant's picture and ripped it up.

"You're not getting away with that, Asa! I want a picture for my album."

"You're welcome to mine. I don't look so hideous in it."

"I think I look pretty cute in them all," Jennifer said.

"We all look good," Grant said. "Only Asa has a vanity problem."

"Maybe I'll improve with age," Asa said. "Break out the food, will you, Patty? I'm starving."

We sat down on the floor to eat. Chicken-salad sandwiches, French fries, cookies, cake, milk, and soda. We ate and talked. The subject was boys, but they were all guys I didn't know, had never even heard of. The conversation went like this:

JENNIFER: What do you think of Michael Gerald?

ASA: Total dink.

GRANT: How about Shaun Cafferelli?

JENNIFER: Cute, cute, *cute.*

GRANT: Francis is a senior.

JENNIFER: I know. That's why I like him, because he's so old.

PATTY: What about Steven Gillespie?

JENNIFER: A-*dor*able!

ASA: Who likes David Zimbee?

JENNIFER: Who doesn't!

After we ate, we got into our pajamas. No one wore anything particularly fashionable. Grant put on an oversized flannel nightshirt and fuzzy elephant slippers. Asa had baggy red footies with a flap seat. Even Patty wore old pj's.

I had brought two pairs of pajamas with me: my favorite old cat pajamas plus a new silky-looking pair Mom had bought me in the thrift shop. They were a little big on me, but Mom said when she saw the initial *S* monogrammed on the pocket, she couldn't resist.

My plan had been to wear the new pajamas if everybody was high-fashion. Instead, I put on my cat pajamas. Jennifer was wearing cat pajamas, too. She pointed at me. "Why do you have cats?"

"Why do you?"

"Because I love cats."

"So do I."

"All *right!*" She flung her arm around my neck, almost choking me. "We cat lovers must stick together."

"How long have you had your cat?" I said, unwinding her arm.

"I do not have *a* cat, Silver. I have *four* cats."

"What are their names, Peter, Paul, and Mary—and Martha?"

"I would never give my cats names like that. Their names are Snowflake, Charcoal, Honeybunch, and Raindrop."

Patty looked up and laughed. Then the door opened again, and again Patty's whole face changed in a flash. "Stay out!" she yelled, as a man walked in.

"Hello, Mr. Dexter," Asa and Grant said almost together. It was Patty's uncle.

"Good evening, young ladies." There was something old-fashioned about him, the way he talked and the way he was dressed, in a stiff, starched shirt with a tie and vest.

"What do you want, Uncle Paul?" Patty said.

"How's everything going, girls? Do you need anything?" He had the same blond hair as Patty's mother, except it was thinner.

"We're fine, you can go," Patty said.

"I hope you all make yourselves at home."

"Oh, we will," Jennifer said. "You know us, Mr. Dexter."

"If anyone wants a midnight snack or anything, go right ahead."

"Okay, okay, they know," Patty said. "Will you leave now?"

I glanced at her. If I ever talked like that to Mom or Cynthia, or even Leo, everybody would scream at me. Mr. Dexter didn't seem to take offense, though. "I stopped in the bakery and bought blueberry muffins for breakfast for you all."

"My favorite kind," Jennifer said. "How ecstatic."

After her uncle left, Patty sat with her eyes closed and her hands clenched. Asa looked at Grant with an expression that said, *There goes Patty into one of her moods again!*

It put a damper on things for a while. We lay

around and read magazines and listened to Suzanne Vega on Patty's tape deck. Then, after a while, Patty seemed to feel okay and everyone cheered up again.

We spread the mattresses on the floor and put on sheets and blankets. "Okay, into beddy-bye," Asa said. She and Jennifer took the bed. Grant, Patty, and I each took a mattress. Patty turned out the lights.

"Hey, wait, there's popcorn in this bed," Asa said.

"Not on my side," Jennifer said.

"Oh, no?"

We could hear Asa sweeping popcorn over to Jennifer's side, then Jennifer throwing it back.

"Help," Asa cried. "SOS!"

The lights went on and the popcorn war started. We scrambled around looking for leftover popcorn to throw at each other. Every time we thought we were out of ammunition, someone would yell "Popcorn alert!" and the battle would start again.

We finally got back in our beds, but we didn't go to sleep. We stayed up, talking. Asa started it. "Let's talk about kissing," she said. "Let's talk about Sarabeth's kiss."

"No," I screamed.

"Yes! We never finished that discussion."

"It was just a kiss, an ordinary kiss."

"Oh, no, you don't get out of it that way. Every kiss is different. I want to rate this kiss. Now, Silver, give us some details. Did he slobber? Was it a wet kiss? Was it a *French* kiss? Did his lips pop when he kissed you? I believe you denied that it was a loud, smacky kiss."

Asa's voice sparkled with mischief. The other three were laughing.

"So, Silver," Asa went on, "was it a quiet little mousy kiss, then? One of those pecky little kisses?"

"Judge Asa, I'm not answering your questions."

"I'll find you in contempt of court."

"I'll cite my constitutional rights."

"I had my first kiss—" Jennifer began.

"—in fourth grade," we all chorused.

Around one o'clock, Patty's mother looked in. "Girls, you're going to be a bunch of wrecks in the morning."

"No, we'll be all right," Grant said.

"Well, I'll be a wreck, staying up thinking about what wrecks *you'll* be." After she left, Patty told me her mother was taking classes at the university so she could become a paralegal. "She really wants to be a lawyer but that's—" I missed the next thing she said. Then I heard her saying, ". . . then we'd have our own money and we wouldn't have to live in my uncle's house."

I think I said, "I didn't know it was his house."

And Patty said, "Well, it is."

"Silver is dozing off," Grant said.

"No . . . I'm not. . . ."

"She always snores like that when she's awake," Asa said.

I wanted to protest, to tell her I didn't snore, but it seemed like too much trouble. The next thing I heard was Asa talking about her older sisters, something about how her family called them "the girls" and Asa "the baby."

"Thaz not so nice," I said.

"Thaz the zilver zombie zpeaking," Grant said.

I heard them laughing, then I heard Patty again, saying something about a bank and her uncle. "Paul thinks because he's an executive, he's an expert on everything. He's such a big shot."

Then Jennifer, "Oh, he's not so bad, Pattycake. He's nice."

"That's what you think," Patty said.

Maybe I dreamed that last bit. I don't remember anything else. I just passed out.

CHAPTER 20

In the morning, Grant and I woke up first, before anyone else. "Where's the bathroom?" I whispered. We took our toothbrushes and tiptoed down the hall, past Patty's uncle's room and her mother's room. Everyone was sleeping.

"Next month we'll have another pj party at Jen's house," Grant said, shutting the bathroom door.

"You'll need the whole month to recover from this one."

Grant laughed. "We get so crazy at these parties, and don't forget we have two more after Jen's. And now with you, it'll be three more."

"Me?" I said, and I thought of the five of us in the trailer. We'd push the walls straight out. But what really flew into my mind was what they would think when they saw where I lived. "Grant, I don't even know if I'll go to Jen's party. She didn't invite me."

"Are we going to go through *that* again? Jen's going to invite you, you'll see."

"Let's talk about it another time."

"I'll just tell you that after Jen's party, we always skip November and December because there's so much other stuff going on—with Thanksgiving, Christmas, and Hanukkah." She ran her toothbrush under the water.

"Hanukkah?" I repeated. "The Jewish holiday?"

"Right. They light candles and give presents."

"I know."

"Good thing, or Jen would jump down your throat for being ignorant."

"I'm always getting on Jennifer's wrong side, anyway."

"Well, you can't blame her about this. It annoys her that people act like there's only Christian holidays in the world." Grant turned on the shower.

"How come Patty lives with her uncle?" I asked.

"Well, he's divorced, and he was living all alone in this big house, and then Patty's mom got divorced, too. She's his sister." Grant stepped into the shower. "Would you put that towel on the hook for me, please, Sarabeth?"

"Sure." I loved the huge, thick towels.

"After Patty's mom was divorced," Grant said, "she had to sell their house. They didn't have any money, and they were living in this awful, freezing place over somebody's garage. So Patty's uncle said they should come live with him."

I flushed the toilet. "Where's Patty's father?"

"Somewhere in Virginia. He has another family now. Patty has a half sister. She goes down to visit about once a year. She says she doesn't even feel like his daughter anymore."

When Grant was done, I got into the shower. "Is it because of her father that Patty gets so moody?"

"I think so," Grant said. She turned on the hair dryer.

"It's funny," I said, "the way all three of us think about our fathers so much."

When we went back, the others were still in bed. "Here we are, clean and beautiful," Grant said.

"You guys are nuts getting up so early," Jennifer said. She yawned. "We're telling our dreams. You missed mine."

"I'm sure their hearts are broken," Asa said.

Patty was telling her dream. "I was running across this green, grassy place. I passed two men singing Spanish songs. One of them was my father."

"I didn't think your father was Spanish," Jennifer said. She had started doing push-ups on the floor.

"Jen, darling, it's a *dream,*" Asa said.

"I tried to talk to him," Patty went on, "but he only spoke Spanish. He didn't understand me. He couldn't hear me . . . he didn't want to hear me."

"Oh!" Asa said.

Patty kept pressing her lips together. "You know what it made me think? When I was small, if something bad happened, all these hands reached out for me. There was always someone around, my parents or my brother or my aunt Louisa. But now it's different. My parents are split. My brother's all the way across the country. My aunt's in Mexico. And I'm supposed to be grown-up, I guess, so I'm lucky if a *finger* reaches out for me."

For a minute no one said anything. All you could hear was Jennifer counting push-ups. Then Asa put a tape on the cassette player.

"Oh, ba-ay-be," a woman sang sadly, "don't do this to meeee, don't do this to meeee, don't do this to meeee, ba-ay-be!"

"Somebody say something cheerful!" Grant ordered.

"Great party, Patty," I said. "I'm really glad I came."

"Our pajama parties are always fun," Jennifer said. "Twenty-two," she counted. "Twenty-three . . ."

But there was still a cloud over everyone. "I didn't know you had an older brother, Patty," I said.

"Bennett," Jennifer said. "He's adorable . . . twenty-seven . . . a ski bum . . . twenty-eight . . . twenty-nine . . . in Vale . . . thirty!" She rolled over, put her hands behind her head, and began to do sit-ups.

"What's a ski bum?"

They all looked at me as if I'd asked what a bread box was.

Jennifer paused in the middle of a sit-up. "You don't know what a ski bum is? A ski bum is someone who all he wants to do is ski, and that's all he does do, and he doesn't have a regular job."

"That describes Bennett," Patty said.

"How does he live?" I asked. "How does he pay his bills?"

"He earns enough money to get along," Patty said. "He teaches skiing and sometimes he'll do other jobs if he needs to. He'll work in a store selling ski stuff or something. . . . Whatever you do, just don't mention him around my uncle Paul. If he gets going on Bennett, it's really boring. Bankers are boring people, anyway." She shook herself, like a dog shaking off water, as if she was shaking off her mood. "Is anybody hungry? Should we get up and go have breakfast?"

"Wait," Grant said. "You have to hear *my* dream. It was so bizarre."

"I didn't know you had a dream," I said. They all looked at me again—the bread-box look. All I'd meant was that Grant hadn't said anything to me when we were in the bathroom together.

"I was swimming," Grant said. "The pool turned into our kitchen. My mother gave me a towel. That turned into a lamp."

"Then what happened?" Jennifer asked.

"Then I woke up, quick, before *I* turned into a teacup."

"My dream was clearly the best," Asa said. "Too bad you guys missed it. I dreamed a gorgeous hunk was kissing me."

Jennifer was still doing sit-ups. "You didn't tell us if he was a good kisser."

"How would I know? You and Sarabeth are the experts."

"Not me," I said. "I don't know anything about kissing."

"Oh, ho, ho," Asa said, "and what about Mark Emelsky?"

"Oh, Mark," I said weakly.

"Oh, Mark," Asa mimicked.

My cheeks got warm. Suddenly I sat up and

said, "I have to make a confession! He never kissed me."

For the third time that morning, they all turned and gave me the bread-box look.

"He didn't kiss you?" Grant said.

I shook my head.

"Not even on the cheek?" Jennifer froze in the middle of a sit-up.

I shook my head again.

"But you told us he kissed you. You told me that," Jennifer said.

"I know what I told you. I'm sorry, it just came out."

"*What* just came out? What are you saying, Sarabeth?"

"Don't jump all over me!"

Jennifer blinked and looked hurt. "*I'm* not the one who's yelling."

"I'll explain everything," I said more calmly. I told them about Mark's phone call and how, afterward, I'd started fooling around with the pillow, making believe it was Mark.

"Weird," Jennifer said.

"Shut up, Jennifer," Asa and Grant said together.

I told them how I'd given Mark The Pillow eyes. I told them everything: about giving Mark The Pillow a mouth so we could kiss and about my mother coming in and almost catching me. Then I told them how, talking to Jennifer in the locker room, saying that Mark had kissed me just popped out of my mouth. "I felt as if it had really happened."

"Well, it did, in a manner of speaking," Grant said loyally.

"If you count being kissed by a pillow," Jennifer said. "And by the way, how was it?"

"Great," I said. "His braces didn't bother me at all."

Asa tossed a bed pillow at me. "Demonstrate! That's your punishment for being sneaky."

"I wasn't sneaky, Asa! I told you, I just got carried away."

"Well, whatever. I want to see the pillow kiss. Right, everybody? We want the pillow kiss, don't we?"

"Yeah, the pillow kiss," Jennifer said. "Show us the pillow kiss."

They all started stamping their feet and chanting, "The pillow kiss, we want the pillow kiss!"

"No, I can't do it," I said. "Mark The Pillow isn't this fat."

"He pigged out on feathers," Asa said. "He gained weight, but he's the same basic, lovable, squeezable Mark The Pillow."

"Mark The Pillow has more character. This guy looks blank."

"Wait a second." Patty went to her desk and came back with a handful of felt-tipped pens.

"You want me to?" I said. "This is a good pillow, isn't it?"

"Go for it, Sarabeth," she said.

I drew eyes, glasses, a mouth.

Patty leaned over my shoulder. "A work of art."

"Who's Art?" Asa was lying on her stomach at the foot of the bed. "I thought his name was Mark."

"Meet Art The Pillow," I said. "Mark The Pillow's brother." I kissed him and fell back on the bed.

"Revive her!" Grant fanned her hand over my face. "Silver's fainted from love of Art The Pillow."

"She fell at his feet," Patty said.

"Blissed out by his cherubic white cheeks," Asa said.

Jennifer grabbed Art The Pillow. "Let someone who knows what she's doing show you amateurs some real kissing." She spun around the room, pressing passionate kisses onto Art The Pillow.

"Lover girl, how come his eyes are still open?" Asa said.

Jennifer threw Art The Pillow across the room. "Kiss him yourself and see if he closes his eyes for you."

Art The Pillow was on the floor. Asa flung herself half off the bed toward him. "My darling one!

My dearest heart! I will soon make you the happiest man in the world."

I guess we were shrieking and making a lot of noise. Someone rapped on the door. Jennifer sat on Art the Pillow. "I hope I don't smother the poor guy," she whispered.

CHAPTER 21

"Lucky for me you're here and not Jennifer," Patty remarked while we were loading the dishwasher.

Grant, Jennifer, and Asa had all gone home right after breakfast. I hadn't expected to be left alone with Patty, and I wasn't too comfortable.

"I wouldn't get two licks' worth of work out of Jen," Patty went on. "That girl hates housework with a passion."

"What's so awful about housework?" My voice got loud.

"I didn't say it was awful, Sarabeth. I just happen to know how Jen feels. There're five kids in her family and Jen's the oldest. She's always getting stuck with the housework."

"Someone has to do it," I said, which was something I'd heard Mom say a thousand times. "Personally, I can't stand people who complain about how horrible and demeaning housework is, how they'd rather do just about anything else. Why don't they say they'd hate being a doctor or a firefighter?"

"Why should they?" Patty argued. "Doctors do something for humanity. Firefighters save lives. Whose life do you save washing dishes? You don't have to go to school to be trained to vacuum a rug or dust a table. You don't even get paid for doing it."

"Patty, there you're wrong. People who do housework as a job get paid."

"Oh. I guess that's true."

"That *is* true, Patty. And another thing, not just anybody can do housework. Anybody can *try,* but that doesn't mean they'll do a good job. There are a lot of things you have to know to do it right. It's hard work. You can't be lazy, and you have to know how to get along with people. There's a lot more to it than you realize!"

"I didn't say *I* hated housework," Patty said. "Mom and I clean this whole house every week." She made a terrible face. "Don't you think that's absurd? My uncle could pay to have someone come in— someone like your mom—but my mom says it's the least we can do. If it was our own house and we had to clean it, I wouldn't mind."

"Or you might not mind doing this one if you got paid."

She slammed the dishwasher shut. "No, I'd never take my uncle's money. I wish I had a job, though. I can't wait to be independent. But what can you do when you're our age, except baby-sit? And around here, there are so many teenage girls, the mothers have their pick, and they always choose the older ones." She started wiping the table. "Sarabeth, what's it like to be poor?"

"Why ask me?" I said. I got the broom and started sweeping the floor. Mom and I didn't have new stuff, and sometimes we had to borrow money, but I didn't think of us as *poor.* "Poor," to me, meant you didn't have a home, you didn't have a place of your own, you didn't have food. That wasn't us.

"I'll tell you what *poor* is," I said. "On TV, I saw this family in New York City with two little kids. They all beg on the subway. They go from one shelter to another. They carry their things in shopping bags and a cart."

"Why don't the parents get jobs?" Patty said.

"The father is sick, he can't work. The mother lost her job and can't get another one. They're just stuck. They spend all their time trying to get money enough for food and a place to sleep at night."

"That's horrible," Patty said.

I was glad she said that. I was afraid she'd say it was the people's own fault, and I knew that would make me mad. "It made me feel sick when I saw it. It made me so angry at the world. I don't think people should have to live like that. It's not fair."

Patty drew down her mouth. "A lot of things aren't fair, Sarabeth. Don't you know that yet?"

Her uncle walked into the kitchen. "Good morning, girls." His hair was damp, and he had a little piece of tissue stuck on his chin where he'd cut himself shaving. He was wearing a dark suit and a striped tie. "Where's the rest of the crew?"

"They went," Patty muttered.

He plugged in the coffeepot. "Did you have a good time at the party?" he asked me. He tousled Patty's hair. She jerked away from him.

"Yes," I said. "It was fun."

"Let me see, your name is Sarah, right?" He gave me a nice smile.

"Sarabeth," I said. "Sarabeth Silver." I started to say "Some people just call me Silver," but the sneer on Patty's face stopped me.

Her mother came in. She was dressed up in a skirt, heels, and a silk blouse. "Are you going to church with Paul and me, Patty?"

"No. Sarabeth has to wait for her mother."

"That's okay," I said. "I can wait outside."

"I'm not going to church," Patty said flatly.

"Mom, I need five dollars. I'm going to the mall later to buy some paints."

"Defacing more walls?" her uncle said.

"You gave me permission." Patty's voice was toneless. "You said as long as I stuck to my room— are you going to go back on your word now?"

Her uncle held up his hands. "Patty darling, I was teasing. A mild little josh." He seemed so patient with Patty, not at all bothered by her moodiness. "I'll get the car ready, Liz," he said to her mother, and he went out to the garage.

"Who are you going to the mall with?" Patty's mother asked.

"I'm going alone."

"You know I don't like you wandering around there alone."

"I wish you could get it through your head that it's perfectly safe," Patty said.

"And I wish you could get it through your head that I am *concerned* about you!"

"Mom, I *know* it's okay for me to be at the mall."

"All right, let's not fight this morning," her mother said. "Try to take it easy, Patty. Easy on me. Easy on yourself. Don't fight the whole world, everything's going to be okay."

"Sure," Patty said. "According to you, everything's terrific." If it was possible to sound bitter, bored, and jaded all at the same time, then Patty managed it. "Come on, Sarabeth, let's go outside."

We were sitting on the steps in front of the house when her uncle backed the car out of the garage. "See you later, darling," he called to Patty. He waved to me. "Wonderful meeting you, Sarabeth."

"Hypocrite, hypocrite, hypocrite," Patty muttered.

We watched the car go down the street.

Neither of us said anything.

Patty shuffled her feet restlessly. Suddenly she said, "Was it hard telling everyone that you faked us out about Mark?"

"In a way, but I didn't think about it too much, actually. I just blurted it out. I'm always blurting things out like that."

"Well, I admire you for saying it." She stared straight ahead, her mouth pinched as if she'd tasted something sour. Had I heard her right? Did she say *admired?* I thought how people kept surprising me. If Patty hadn't said that, I would have been positive the sour look was meant for me.

"I felt like a fool," I said. "I didn't want you to think I was a liar or something cheap and crummy like that."

"You mean about Mark The Pillow?" Her mouth relaxed and she almost smiled. "That wasn't a real lie, Silver."

"It wasn't exactly the truth, either," I said.

"Real lying is mean," Patty said, looking at me intently. "Real lying is hurting somebody. You didn't hurt anyone. You made something up. Mark The Pillow. It made you happy. I don't see how that can be bad." She leaned toward me. "How about when something bad—I mean really bad—happens? What's the worst thing that's ever happened in your life?"

"My father." I told her about the tires flying off the truck.

"No, I didn't mean that kind of thing. There are other things that happen to people that aren't sad—they're awful, evil, and you can't tell any-body—" She broke off, and her mouth got that sour, unhappy expression again.

I wondered what could be so awful in Patty's life. There was her parents' divorce—that was seri-ous, but still . . . She'd used the word *evil*. I looked around at the quiet street, the trees and lawns, kids riding by on bikes. Then I looked at Patty. She was wearing leather pants, little red boots, a thin gold chain around her neck with her initials in gold dan-gling from it. P. A. L. Patricia Andrea Lewis. Even her name was elegant. She had everything going for her.

"Sometimes things happen that you wish you had made up," Patty said, "but they're real, and you can't even tell anybody." Her voice was flat again, but she kept blinking, and I thought she was close to tears.

"Why can't you tell anybody? Can't you tell your mom?"

Patty looked down at her hands. "You saw the way she is. She doesn't believe anything I say."

"No, Patty, I'm sure if you—"

"Forget it, please. Forget I said anything."

I tried to put my arm around her, but her whole body was stiff. It was like trying to hug a wall. It made me feel sorry for her. "I know you have Grant and the others, Patty," I said, "but if you ever need me for anything—"

"Sure." She cut me off.

I leaned back on the steps. As usual, I'd said too much.

We sat in silence for a few minutes. And then, just as I heard our car coming down the block, Patty said, "I'll remember that, Silver. I really will."

CHAPTER 22

Grant had tickets to a flute and piano concert at Irving Hall, the music building on the college campus. "Who wants to go with me?" she asked at lunch. "It's a school night, but you won't get home too late. It starts early."

Patty shook her head.

I said I didn't have a ride.

"Not me," Jennifer said. "I always fall asleep at concerts."

Asa opened her Reading Arts anthology.

No one wanted to go. Grant looked so disappointed, I said I'd get a ride somehow and go with her.

"Thanks, Silver. You're a true friend."

"You'll be a *sor-ry* friend," Jennifer sang out.

"Take a good book or even a dull book, to avoid total tedium," Asa advised.

"You guys are a bunch of barbarians," Grant said. "Flute and piano are two of the most beautiful instruments!"

"Yeah, we got no culture," Jennifer said.

Mom was working late the night of the concert, so Cynthia drove me over to the campus. Grant's mother had said she'd pick us up afterward. "I'm glad of that," Cynthia said. "Now I can go home and tumble into bed. I have a splitting headache."

"Is it one of your tension headaches?"

"Probably."

"Why are you tense?"

"I don't want to work for a while after the baby comes, so we might be tight on money. I keep trying to figure things out, and then I end up with a headache." She pulled up in front of the steep sidewalk to Irving Hall. "Where's your friend? I can't park here, but it's probably okay to stand for a while."

I spotted Grant sitting on the stone steps of the building and waved out the window. "She's up there, the blonde girl."

Cynthia put her hand on my shoulder and peered out the window. "Which one? There are two blonde girls up there."

Then I saw Patty. So she was here, too! I felt a

stab of disappointment—I'd thought I'd be alone with Grant.

I still liked being alone with her best. Sometimes, though, when we were all together, I felt awkward and touchy even with Grant. The easy, familiar way the four of them were with each other always reminded me of how different I was from them. I didn't have their money. I didn't have their memories. They had known each other forever. They were like a plant with their roots all tangled together. They went way back to "when," that *when* someone was always starting a sentence with—*Remember when we . . .*

Patty and Grant walked down to meet me. "I didn't know you were coming, Patty," I said.

"She changed her mind at the last minute," Grant said. She put her arm through mine.

Irving Hall was an old building with thick limestone walls and mullioned windows. Inside it was cool and high-ceilinged, with scuffed hardwood floors. There were about fifty people at the concert. We sat upstairs in the curve of the balcony because Grant said the acoustics were best there.

I had come to the concert for Grant's sake, but I ended up liking it more than I thought I would, especially the solo flute. Grant sat forward, listening intently, barely moving. Patty sat quietly, too, only there was something knotted and edgy in her quietness. I caught her eye once. She blinked, looked like she was waking up, and gave me a wavery little smile.

At intermission, Grant said she was going to try to talk to Nina Bauler, the flutist. "Should I ask for her autograph?" she said. "Well, I will," she decided.

"Is she famous?" I asked.

"Not yet." Grant went off backstage. Patty and I went to the women's room.

We were washing our hands and I was saying something about school—I don't remember what—when I looked at Patty and saw that she was crying. She was standing there with her hands under running water, and tears were falling down her cheeks.

"Patty, are you sick? What's the matter?"

"Oh God," she whispered on a gulp of breath, "oh God, oh God, oh God."

"Patty—"

She hung on to the basin. "Oh God, oh God, oh God, oh God."

I started to get scared. "Patty? What is it, Patty? Should I get you something? Should I get Grant?" I wet a paper towel and wiped her face. "Patty, come on. . . ." I tried to think what to do. What would Cynthia do? Put her arms around Patty. Encourage her to talk.

I put my arms around her. "Patty, honey, can you tell me?"

She was whimpering. "I've got to talk to somebody. . . . Got to . . ." And then in a rush, a whisper, "Sarabeth, it's him."

"Him?"

"It's him," she said urgently, staring at me. Her eyes seemed to stick out of her head. "It's *him.*"

"Who? What are you talking about?"

"Paul," she said.

"Your uncle Paul?"

"*Yes.*"

"What about him?"

"I hate him," she said, as if that explained everything. "I hate him. I hate him so much." She started to breathe hard. "I can't get my breath! Sarabeth, I can't breathe!"

I held her. She was gasping and choking. I kept thinking I should get Grant, somebody, but I didn't want to leave Patty alone.

"Always staring at me," she said. "Always telling me how beautiful I am."

She was leaning on me. She was heavy. "You want to sit down?" I asked.

She wiped her nose. "Why am I telling *you?*"

"Do you want me to get Grant?" I asked again.

"No! Don't leave! Help me! No, you can't! Nobody can help me. He's doing things."

"Things?"

"Things," she said hoarsely. "Don't you understand *anything?* He's doing things to me."

"What things?" I said, but I already half knew.

She told me about her uncle Paul, told me this stuff that I'd never heard anybody real say. I'd read about it in the newspapers and I'd heard about it on TV, but this was different. This was Patty saying these things about her uncle.

Her uncle Paul! I'd met him. I knew him. I'd shaken his hand, talked to him, eaten food he'd brought into the house.

And now Patty was saying these things about him, her own uncle, her uncle Paul who'd asked "Did you have a good time at the party?" . . . Who'd said, "I bought blueberry muffins for you girls."

Patty's arm was touching my arm. I could feel how warm her skin was. And she was saying these things.

"He comes in my room. He sits on the bed. He asks me about school and my friends and he says, 'Sit with me.' I don't want to, but he just keeps asking in this way he has, as if he's so nice, and he never gives up. 'Sit with me. Sit with me, Patty. Don't be standoffish. Sit with me.' So I do it. I sit with him, just so he'll leave me alone. At first he just rubbed my back or my arms. I didn't like it, but I let him. Then he started other things. And he told me never to tell my mother because if I did, we'd have to leave his house. I thought to myself, *Oh, please, yes, let's leave, let's go away from here.* I asked Mom where we'd go if we left Uncle Paul's and she said, 'Why would we leave? It would be a disaster. We don't have any money.' She would have to drop out of school."

I thought if this had happened to me, I would be screaming. But Patty was talking in a low voice, a quiet, dull voice, and her face was smooth and squashed-looking, as if she'd pulled a sheet of plastic over it.

"What about your mother?" I said. "Didn't you tell her?"

"I did. I tried to tell her, but it was like I was saying one thing and she was hearing something else. She keeps saying she knows I'm not happy about the divorce and that I'm sensitive and she knows it isn't easy living with somebody else." She wiped her eyes with a paper towel. "Do you want to hear this crazy stuff? You'll miss the concert."

"I don't care about the concert, Patty." We stayed in there, talking. Faintly, in the background, I heard the music start again.

Suddenly Patty flung her arms around me. "Sarabeth, help me. What should I do? Tell me what to do."

"Patty, I will. I promise, I'll help you." She

sounded so desperate, I hugged her as tight as I could.

She washed her face and looked at herself in the mirror, and she tried to make a joke. "Patty, the red-eyed witch."

"No, you look beautiful."

"Don't say that! I *hate* hearing that. I hate hearing I'm beautiful. It's what *he* says all the time."

The door to the women's room opened, and Grant came in. "Patty? Sarabeth?" she called. Then she saw us. "What are you doing? The concert—" She stared at Patty. "What's the *matter?*"

When Grant heard Patty's story, she started crying.

After a while we went outside and sat on the steps. It was dark and chilly. There were lights on here and there on the campus. A wind blew and leaves fell. We sat close together, with Patty in the middle. And we talked about what Patty could do, who she could tell.

"What about Grant's mother?" I suggested.

"I don't know. . . . Maybe . . ."

"Or Asa's father, Judge Goronkian?"

"You don't know what you're saying, Sarabeth," Patty said. "Judge Goronkian and my uncle and some other men eat lunch together every Tuesday. They're all friends. Anyway, all my uncle has to do is say I'm imagining things. That's what he told Mom. He said he would gladly pay for therapy for me."

"Therapy? You mean, like you're crazy?" Grant said.

Patty nodded. " 'Very confused' is what he says. They'll believe him before they believe me. I'm just a kid. He's someone important."

"You have to do something," I said. "Lock your door."

"I thought of that. No locks."

"Talk to your mom again. Just try it."

"Sarabeth, Paul is her brother, and she thinks he's the sun and the moon. He took us in when we needed help. She says I don't give him a chance. She says he loves me and it's not a crime for him to come into my room. It's his house."

"Yes, but what he did—I bet that's a crime!"

Patty looked down.

"What about your brother?" Grant said.

"What about him? He's in Colorado."

A horn tooted. A black car was parked at the bottom of the walk. "Grant, I thought your mother was coming for us," Patty said.

"She is."

"Then why's my uncle here?"

"Your uncle?" Grant said, putting her hand to her eyes.

The car door opened, and Patty's uncle Paul got out and waved to us to come down.

CHAPTER 23

"Where's my mother, Mr. Dexter?" Grant asked. We all got in the backseat.

"She called and said something had come up. ... Where do you live, Sarabeth?"

I gave him directions and he pulled into traffic.

I was sitting behind him. I kept looking at the back of his head. It seemed unreal that he was the same man Patty had told us about. Everything about him was so normal. He was wearing a tweed jacket. He yawned and rubbed his head. He ate a Lifesaver, passed the package back to us, and said, "My favorite candy is chocolate, but I can't let myself eat too much of it or I put on the pounds."

Patty passed me a note: I DON'T WANT TO DRIVE HOME ALONE WITH HIM. PASS IT ON.

Of course! After her uncle dropped me off, he would take Grant home, and then he and Patty would be alone. I passed the note to Grant.

"What are we going to do?" she mouthed.

I did the first thing that came to my mind. "Mr. Dexter." I leaned toward the front seat. "Patty is feeling sort of sick. Could you take her home first, please? Before me?"

"What's the matter, Patty?" her uncle said.

She looked at me. "I'm nauseous."

"You should have told me. We'll get you right home." He U-turned.

When we got to Patty's house, Grant got out with her. "I'm going to call Mom and see if I can stay overnight," she said.

I thought that was brilliant. Her uncle couldn't bother Patty if Grant was there. I waved goodbye to them and settled back in the seat. Then, as Patty's uncle pulled away, I saw on Grant's face that she had just thought of the same thing that I had. Now *I* was alone in the car with him.

I sat on the edge of the seat, my hand on the door. I'd jump out if he tried anything. I started talking to him in my mind, yelling at him that I knew what he was doing to Patty and he should leave her alone. If only I had the nerve to say it! But would he listen to me? Would he care one fig for anything I said? Like Patty said, we were kids. He was a grown-up. An adult. A man. He looked so solid, so big, so important. Telling him off would be like yelling at a policeman.

"Would you like an ice cream, Sarabeth?"

I jumped. "Excuse me?"

"Would you like an ice cream?"

"No. Thank you."

He drove into the parking lot of a dairy bar and parked under a tree. There was only one other car in the lot, way over on the other side. "I've got a yen for something sweet," he said. He turned off the key and looked at me. It was dark and shadowy in the car. His head looked enormous, his eyes were dark spots in his face. "You sure you don't want something?"

"No." My jaw was so tight the muscles in my cheeks ached.

He went into the dairy bar. I could see him through the window, talking to the girls behind the counter. They were laughing. I thought about getting out of the car and walking home. Was that crazy? Or was it crazy to stay in the car? I slid over toward the door. Should I do it? I jumped out and walked away fast.

"Sarabeth."

I was at the edge of the parking lot. I turned around, my heart banging against my ribs.

Patty's uncle walked toward me, licking an ice-cream cone. "Getting a little fresh air? You still have time to change your mind about the ice cream." He held his cone out to me. "Try it," he said. "It's a new flavor."

"No, I don't want any."

"Too bad, you're missing something." He held the door to the front seat open, but I got in the back again. "You could sit up front," he said.

"No, that's okay. Thank you."

He smiled. "You kids are funny."

All the way back to Roadview, he talked to me about chocolate. "It's my big weakness," he said. "I could sit down and eat a huge bar of chocolate all by myself. The best chocolate is made in Europe. Here, we put too much sugar in it and the ingredients aren't as pure." Then he told me a joke, something about the difference between people who eat chocolate and people who jog.

"I don't get it," I said.

"It's very silly." He never really explained it because he started laughing. Anyway, it was hard for me to listen—I was too tense. But when he laughed, I did, too.

When he pulled up in front of our trailer, my hands were so cramped I could hardly open the door.

"Push the handle down," he said.

I got out of the car. "Thank you for the ride."

"You're entirely welcome. I think that's your mother at the window."

"Yes, she's waiting for me." I ran up the path.

CHAPTER 24

"How'd it go?" Grant said in homeroom the next morning. "Were you all right?"

I told her about stopping for ice cream. "I was so nervous! And I couldn't sleep last night for thinking about Patty."

"You look tired," Grant said sympathetically.

"What about you and Patty?" I asked.

"Oh, no problems." She wrinkled her nose like she was going to sneeze. "Naturally! I was right there with her, so he couldn't—"

"Are you going to sleep over again?"

She sneezed. "Excuse me. . . . Maybe I will, but I can't sleep over every night. . . . What are we going to do, Silver?"

"Do you think somebody has written advice about this stuff for kids?"

"I don't know," Grant said. "Want to meet me at the library at lunchtime?"

"What'll we tell the others about not eating with them?"

"We'll say we have a research project." She sneezed several times more.

"Are you getting a cold?"

"I have weird allergies. I've been sneezing ever since I went into Patty's house. I'm probably allergic to her uncle."

The first thing we did in the library was go to the card catalog. I stood at Grant's side, watching and half shielding her while she flipped through the cards. We couldn't find anything under Sex Abuse. "Try Sex Education," I whispered.

"Okay." We were both whispering.

"Maybe there are no books about it. Some people think we're just too young and innocent to know about sex."

"Yes, we don't know the terrible things in life. We're just sweet and protected."

"And only good things happen to us," I added. We started to laugh at how sarcastic we were being. Then I think we both had the same thought at the same moment. *We're joking, and Patty's in trouble.*

"Let's ask Mrs. Packwood," Grant said.

I looked over at the librarian doubtfully. "What's she like?"

"She's great. Everyone says so."

Mrs. Packwood's black hair was parted on the side. She was wearing a white blouse that was coming out of her skirt and a wide, unknotted paisley tie around her neck. She was standing on the sides of her shoes, talking to some boys. One of them reminded me of Mark—glasses and braces. "Now, Brian," Mrs. Packwood said to him, "you can't fool me that way." She laughed.

"Hello, Mrs. Packwood," Grant said.

"Hello, Grant. Glad to see you in the library again. Looking for something special?"

"Oh . . ."

Grant and I looked at each other. And again we had the same thought. We weren't going to say anything.

We wandered around in the stacks, looking at the labels on the shelves: FICTION, HISTORY, BIOGRAPHY, SCIENCE, SPORTS. Everything but what we wanted.

"I'm discouraged," Grant said, sneezing.

"I'm hungry," I said. "We missed our lunch for nothing." But a minute later, I found a label that said HEALTH AND SEX ED.

There were three books on the shelf and they all looked old and dusty. The freshest thing there was a typewritten sign:

STUDENTS, IF YOU WANT TO READ

THESE BOOKS ON HEALTH AND SEX EDU-
CATION MATTERS (AND I WANT YOU TO
READ THEM), THEN PLEASE DO THE FOL-
LOWING:

1. <u>CHECK</u> THE BOOKS OUT; DO NOT
JUST TAKE THEM.

2. RETURN THE BOOKS WHEN YOU ARE
DONE SO OTHER PEOPLE CAN READ THEM,
TOO.

3. <u>PLEASE DON'T HIDE THE BOOKS
WHEN YOU ARE THROUGH READING
THEM.</u>

THANK YOU FOR COOPERATING.

LUCY PACKWOOD

Grant took down one of the books and opened it.
"I think they wrote this when dinosaurs roamed the
earth."

I looked over her shoulder as she checked the
table of contents and then the index. "Nothing on
what we want," she said. "But if you're interested
in how the chicken lays eggs, there's a whole chapter
in here."

A group of boys sat down at a table at the end
of the aisle and started talking in loud voices.

"Just what we needed," I said.

"Ignore them," Grant whispered.

The boys looked over at us, and one of them
waved. "Hi, dollies."

"Where do they learn stupid things like that?" Grant said. "I suppose *he'd* like to be called a 'dollie'?" She glared at the boy. I was glad the boy who looked like Mark wasn't with them.

I pulled out another book and went through the table of contents. Nothing about sex abuse. I turned to the back of the book. There wasn't even an index in this one.

"We're wasting our time, Silver," Grant said and sneezed four times in a row.

"Gesundheit," one of the boys said.

"God bless you," another one said.

"Does she need a tissue?"

"No, she needs a flu shot."

"Maybe she needs a shot in the head."

Grant rolled her eyes at me and took down the last of the three books.

Suddenly one of the boys made what Mom calls "a rude noise and a ruder smell," and they all jumped up, cackling like a bunch of hens and saying things like, "Let me out of here. . . . Where's the fresh air. . . . Evacuate the area!"

Grant and I looked at each other again. Here we were, doing this serious, really important thing for Patty, and now *this*. We started giggling and couldn't stop.

CHAPTER 25

I saw Brian, Mark's look-alike, twice more that afternoon, once coming out of the Guidance Office and another time going up the second-floor stairs. It was really strange because I'd never noticed him before, and now, all of a sudden, I seemed to see him everywhere. I guess, because of that, I was thinking about Mark when I got home from school. When the phone rang I was convinced it was Mark. "Hello. Hello! I knew you were going to call," I said.

"You did?" Leo said.

"Oh. Leo."

"Who were you expecting?"

"Nobody special."

"That's who you got," Leo said. "Listen, tell your mom to call me when she gets in."

"Sure."

"Tell her I love her."

"Sure."

"Tell her I plan to give her the first million I make."

"Sure."

"You won't forget?"

"As soon as she walks in the door, Leo!"

"Very good. Got to get back to work."

After Leo hung up, I drank a glass of milk. Why *hadn't* Mark called me? Maybe he had and I'd missed the calls. Or maybe he was waiting for me to call him. Did he really think I was a great person, like he'd told Patty?

I wandered into the living room and turned on the TV. Tobias settled himself on my foot. On the screen, a woman with dark made-up eyes threw herself across a couch and pounded it. "Oh, oh, oh," she cried, "I miss him! I miss him so much!"

"Me, too," I told her.

"Why doesn't he call me?" she wailed.

"Maybe he's waiting for *you* to call him?" I suggested.

"Does he think of me at all?" she asked, sitting up.

"I wish I could tell you he did," I said sympathetically, "but I don't want to give you false hopes."

"I can't go on this way!" She started tearing at her hair.

"Take it easy," I said. "You'll need a wig if you don't stop doing that!"

She staggered across the room, stopped in front of a mirror, and stared at herself for a long time. Her eyes filled with tears.

A shiver went down my back. It was very emotional.

Music came up, the picture faded, and a commercial came on. A man in a white suit was sitting at a table eating a plate of spaghetti covered with blood-red sauce. "Ciao," he said, smiling, "if you want a little taste of heaven—"

I turned off the TV and went back into the kitchen. I dialed Mark's number.

"Hello? Emelskys'," a girl said.

"May I speak to Mark, please?" I tried to make my voice like Grant's, calm and unruffled.

"Mark," the girl screamed, "one of your ditzy girlfriends is on the phone."

One of his girlfriends? What did that mean?

Then Mark was there. "Hello?"

"Hi . . . Mark? It's me. Silver."

"Who?"

My cheeks started burning. "It's Sarabeth," I said. "Sarabeth Silver."

"Oh. Sarabeth! Hi."

"Were you expecting somebody else to call?"

"No. Why?"

"Oooh . . . nothing. No reason."

"Hey, how are you?"

"I'm just fine, Mark. How about you?"

"Yeah, good. What're you doing?"

"Not much. Going to school. . . . You know, the usual. I went to a concert last night at the college."

"The flute concert? My father went to that. He said it was pretty good."

"Yes, it was. It was good."

"Well, gee . . . this is nice, Sarabeth. I was pretty surprised to hear your voice."

"You were? How come? Did you forget what I sound like?"

"No, not that, I just haven't heard from you or anything."

"Well, that's true. I've been busy."

"Me, too," he said.

All of a sudden there was this long, loud silence. I couldn't think of a thing to say and I guess Mark couldn't, either. What had we talked about the other times? Cats? Music? Whales?

"I was just thinking," he said, "maybe you'd like to go someplace with me tonight."

"Oh, sure!" Did I accept too fast? Did I sound too enthusiastic? "The movies?" I blurted.

"No, my sister Kate is playing basketball tonight in the Youth Basketball Program and Mom and I were going to go cheer her on. I thought maybe you'd like to—"

"Oh, sure," I said again, quickly. His mom? Was that a date if I went out with him and his mom? "Where's it going to be?"

"At your school."

"DSD?"

"Right."

"I'll have to ask my mother if she can drive me over."

"Great," he said. "Meet you there at seven."

When Mom came home, she was pretty negative. "You want to go out *again?* Sarabeth, it's a school night."

"I don't think it'll be very late."

"And then I have to pick you up, too."

"Mom, couldn't you go see Leo or something?" That reminded me of his message. "He wants you to call him. He says he loves you and you get his first million."

Mom kicked off her sneakers. Now she was laughing. *Thanks, Leo,* I thought.

"Who is this boy, anyway? Somebody from your school?" she asked.

"Remember the boy who walked me out of the school dance?"

Mom nodded and made glasses over her nose with her fingers. "Cute little boy."

"Mom, he's not little."

"Well, you know what I mean. . . . What're we going to have for supper?"

"Do I always have to decide?"

"It's fine if you want to leave it up to me, but you know me, hon. I don't have a lot of imagination about food." She opened the refrigerator. "How about cheese sandwiches?"

"Fine! I'm not hungry, anyway," I said. And I wasn't. My stomach was rocking around, just thinking about seeing Mark.

"Come on, baby," one of the mothers shouted. "Teamwork, teamwork, teamwork!"

"Which one's her kid?" I whispered to Mark.

He gestured. "That redheaded boy. . . . Come on, Katie," he shouted to his sister. "Dribble that ball. You can do it."

My "date" with Mark was in the school gym. We were sitting on the floor on mats with about a dozen other people, parents and sibs of the kids playing basketball. Mrs. Emelsky was on the other side of Mark. She was wearing jeans, sneakers, and a Norwegian sweater over a turtleneck. I breathed a prayer of thanks that this time I wasn't dressed wrong. I'd worn jeans and a sweat shirt, even though Mom had tried to get me to dress up. And I'd braided my hair. Mom had wanted me to curl it with the curling iron. *Boy, were you ever wrong, Mom.*

I'd tell her that as soon as she picked me up.

"Go, Katie!" Mark yelled. "Show 'em stuff!"

Katie Emelsky was the only girl on her team. She was cute. She was wearing white shorts, a white T-shirt, and a big white bow in the back of her hair. The other team had two girls, and they were beating Katie's team.

A girl who'd been hanging around the entrance to the gym walked toward us. She had an expectant, smile on her face. "Hi, Mark," she said. She had reddish-blonde hair and very fine, nearly white eyebrows. It made her lips look startlingly red. "Long time no see, Mark." She glanced at me.

"Hey!" he said, jumping up. "Pamela! Wow, I can't believe this! Long time no see is right. What are you doing here?"

"The Camera Club was meeting. I was just leaving, and I looked in here and saw you. You've grown up, haven't you?" She tapped him on the nose.

Camera Club . . . That meant she went to DSD, but I didn't recognize her. There were hundreds of kids I didn't know. She looked older than me, older than Mark. I tried not to stare too obviously. She was the sort of person you *wanted* to keep staring at, to try to figure out why she was so interesting-looking.

"Hello, Mrs. E.," she said. "Remember me?"

She leaned over, smiling, and touched Mark's mother on the arm.

Mrs. Emelsky turned. "Well, of course I remember you, Pamela. How *are* you? You're looking great."

"Thanks! You, too."

Mark got up and walked to the entrance with Pamela. I knew I shouldn't, but I felt jealous. Mrs. Emelsky hadn't talked to *me* like that: *How are you!* She'd said, "Hello, Sarabeth. Nice to meet you." Perfectly polite and completely uninterested. Mrs. Emelsky hardly knew me. What did I expect her to do, throw her arms around me? But she had, nearly, with the white-eyebrowed girl.

The gym was stifling, and at halftime, Mark and I went outside the building and walked around. I wanted to ask him about Pamela—where he knew her from, how old she was, what kind of friends they were. We talked about everything *but* Pamela—his sister Katie and basketball and our cats. I told him about Tobias bringing mice into the kitchen and eating them on the scatter rug.

"Well, why not?" Mark said. "It's his home, too."

I laughed. I liked Mark more than ever.

We passed the library and I thought about Patty and being in there with Grant. "Did you ever hear about a girl being abused?" I said.

"What girl?"

"No particular girl. I just meant, in general, did you ever hear of it?"

"Sure. Boys get abused, too."

"I think it's the most horrible thing in the world," I said.

"It's pretty bad, I guess, but maybe there are worse things."

"Not if it's happening to you," I argued. "When it's happening to you, it has to be the worst thing in the world."

"Maybe you're right," he said.

We went back in to watch the second half of the game. Katie's team was still losing. "Come on, Katie," Mark shouted.

"Come on, Katie!" I shouted.

Mark looked over at me, smiling. Then his face got very serious, and he leaned close to me and said in a soft voice for only me to hear, "Sarabeth, were you talking about yourself?"

"When?" I said. "I'm always talking about myself. I think I talk about myself too much."

"No you don't," he said. He kept saying things that made me like him more. "I mean before, when we were outside and we were talking about girls being—"

"Oh, no!" I said. "Not me. I don't have a father or an uncle, even. It's just Mom and me."

"Your mom was with a man the night of the dance," he remembered.

"That was Leo," I said. "No, not Leo. Oh, no, no."

He leaned against me. "Okay. That's good."

Yeah, good for me, but what about Patty? It made me sad. But I pushed the sadness away because I couldn't do anything for Patty just then.

Katie's team lost. "Phooey!" she said, coming off the court and sitting down next to her mother.

"Sweetie," Mrs. Emelsky said, "who wins or loses isn't supposed to matter. It was a close game, anyway."

"I wanted to win." Katie put her head in her mother's lap. She was ten years old. She glanced up at me. "Did you call Mark today?"

"Yes. Did you answer the phone?"

She got this little devilish smile. "Yeah." I could almost see her remembering how she'd yelled for Mark: *One of your ditzy girlfriends. . . .*

I gave her back a nice, big-sisterly kind of smile. I was sure a lot of other girls liked Mark, and maybe they called him up and maybe they hoped they were his girlfriends, but to be perfectly honest, I was also sure from the way he talked to me and looked at me that *I* was the one he liked most. Or almost sure, anyway. There was that girl with the white eyebrows. Pamela. He'd given her a lot of soft, admiring looks. Still, I didn't worry about her too much. She was too old for him. Besides, I liked Mark more and better than any boy I'd ever known. So maybe it just had to be . . . Mark and me.

Mrs. Emelsky took us all out for ice cream at Friendly's. I called Mom at Leo's a little while after we got there, and she told me to wait outside for her.

"I'll be there in half an hour."

"Don't rush, Mom."

I went back to the table. "Mark was just telling me about your cat, Sarabeth," his mother said. "Does he really weigh fifteen pounds?"

"He needs to go to a fat farm," Katie said.

"He's not fat," I said. "He's big."

"That's right, be loyal to your cat," Mrs. Emelsky said.

Katie rolled her eyes.

When I got up to go, Mark got up, too. "I'll wait outside with you, Sarabeth."

I thanked Mrs. Emelsky for the ice cream. "You're welcome, Sarabeth. I liked meeting you. I hope I see you again." She shook my hand and gave me a very nice smile.

"See you sometime," Katie said. "Or maybe not," she added, in a bratty drawl.

I had a childish impulse to thumb my nose at her. *Nyaaa, nyaaa, nyaaa, can't you see your brother likes me?*

Outside, we stood against the building. Our hands touched. I turned my head toward Mark. I could smell his shampoo, and my stomach did a funny thing—it sort of fell in as if I were sick, except I didn't feel bad, I felt wonderful, and I wanted to kiss him.

Do it, I thought. Pretend he's Mark The Pillow. He'll like it. And so will you.

Mark looked at me. Our faces were really close.

My cheeks were blazing. I couldn't make myself do it.

And then *he* did it. He kissed me. He leaned toward me and touched his lips to mine. He held my hand hard and kept his mouth on my mouth.

A horn honked somewhere. *Baap, baap, baap.*

I was lost, dizzy, and the sound of the horn seemed to come from a distance.

Baap, baap, baap.

Baap, baap, baap.

CHAPTER 26

A few mornings later, right after I got off the bus, I saw Patty sitting on the steps outside the gym, her arms wound around her legs. I waved and went over to her. "Are you going in?"

She didn't respond. She didn't look up.

The bell rang. "Patty?" She didn't move. "Patty, we're going to be late."

Her head sank lower onto her arms.

I bent over her. "Patty, what's the matter? Did something happen with—"

"Oh, God, Silver," she mumbled, "I think I'm going crazy." She stood up and sort of stumbled or swayed, and then she walked away.

I hesitated. I wasn't sure what I should do. I looked around, but the grounds were empty. Everyone was inside. I ran after Patty. "Are you going somewhere?"

"I don't know. No. Nowhere." There was something terrible about her appearance—a blank, squashed-flat look on her face.

"Come on, don't you want to go back to school?"

"Go away, Silver. Go to school. Leave me alone."

I took her hand. It was limp, clammy. She was like somebody who'd been in an accident. I thought she might do anything: walk into the street in front of a car, fall down and bang her head against the sidewalk, or start screaming and tearing off her clothes.

"I'll go with you," I said.

"Where?"

"Wherever you're going."

We walked up into the hilly residential section around the school. I had my books and my lunch in my knapsack. I took out a banana and peeled it. "Have some," I said.

"No."

"Come on, just a bite," I insisted. It seemed to me that eating a banana was such a normal thing to do that maybe it would make Patty feel better. I took the first bite off the top of the banana to encourage her. She took a piece and ate it, then she ate the rest of it, gulped it down, really wolfed it down.

"Did you eat breakfast?" I asked.

"I don't think so."

"Don't you remember?"

"No, I didn't. I didn't eat. I just left the house."

"This is your lucky day, then." She gave me a look from the corner of her eyes. "Well, I mean, in some ways," I said quickly. "Like this." I took out my sandwich and handed it to her. "Cheese and tomato. A great combo."

She ate the sandwich, and she ate the apple I'd brought, and then we shared the cookies.

"Don't you love fall?" I said. The trees were starting to turn color. "It's my favorite season."

"I hate it."

That killed conversation for a while.

We went around the corner of Harker Avenue and started down the hill. At the bottom, there was a little grocery store. "I'm thirsty," Patty said. We went in. The woman behind the counter wore a white apron. The store was tiny and lined from floor to ceiling with shelves filled with everything you could think of. "What do you want?" I asked Patty.

"I don't care."

"Two orange sodas, please," I said. I thought of Mark for a moment. Orange sodas . . . and the dance . . . and his kiss the other night. I hadn't told anyone yet.

The woman looked at us curiously. "No school today, girls?"

"My friend isn't feeling well," I said. "I'm taking her home."

"I thought it was something like that." You could tell from the way she said it that she was the kind of person who always liked to be right. She handed us the sodas. "If you drink that here, you can just give me back the bottles." She pointed to the broad sill in the front window. "Sit down over there."

We sipped our sodas. There was sun in the window. It was cozy. The phone rang, and the woman went in the back of the store and started a long conversation.

The sun made me want to close my eyes. Mark slid into my mind again. The parking lot . . . *Baap, baap, baap. . . .*

"Sarabeth." Patty pinched my arm.

My eyes opened. "What?"

"Remember the concert? Ever since, I've been thinking how to make Mom believe me about my uncle."

"Has he been bothering you again?"

Patty gave me a bitter look. "What do you think!" She shifted closer to me. "Last night, I told my mother—"

"You told her everything?"

"No! I told you, I've tried that before. I told

her Uncle Paul unsnapped my pajamas. I thought, *One thing, just tell her one thing. Just get her to listen.* She did, too. She said—she asked me to repeat what I said. Then she said, 'Okay, let's go, and you say that in front of your uncle.' "

A fly buzzed in the window. The woman in the white apron was still on the phone.

"My uncle was in the living room, having a drink. He always has a glass of sherry before supper. He was sitting in his chair, having his drink and watching TV, and Mom said, 'I'm sorry to disturb you, Paul, but I want you to listen to this and tell me what you think of it.' The way she said that got me really upset. *Tell me what you think of it?* I was so upset I said it wrong. I said that he *pulled* my pajamas."

"It's not that much different," I said.

"Oh, it is, Sarabeth. My mother said, 'You didn't say *that* before.' And my uncle put on this sorrowful face, he acted so surprised and shocked and disturbed about me. He said *of course* he never did any such a thing. Pulled my pajamas? No! He never did it and I knew it." Patty wiped the mouth of the bottle and gulped down the last drop of the soda.

"Then Mom said, 'Well, Patty?' I tried to explain to her that I'd gotten confused and said it wrong. I tried to explain that he was doing these things. Mom said, 'Oh, Patty, Patty,' really unhappy, like I was the most disappointing thing in her life.

"And my uncle said he was truly sorry I was such a muddled person and that my mind was such a jumbled place."

Patty's voice dropped away. It was so low I had to move closer to hear her. "I started crying. I didn't want to, but I couldn't help myself. Mom had class and had to leave. She didn't have time to eat supper because of me bringing this up. She told me I should go to my room and calm down and think about things, think about other people and how hard they work and how selfish it was of me to disrupt everyone's life."

Patty stopped and leaned her forehead against the window. I put my hand over hers.

"And then—" She stopped and swallowed. "Mom went out. I went up to my room and sat down at my desk. I did try to get calm. I thought I would do homework, get my mind on something else. Uncle Paul came up and asked if I wanted supper. I said no. He said I should eat, that he was worried about me. He said it wasn't very nice of me to tell lies about him. I closed my eyes. I thought, *When I open my eyes, he'll be gone.*

"I opened my eyes and he was sitting on my bed. I said, 'Please get out. Please leave my room.'

He didn't move. He said he wanted us to be friends—that that's all he wanted—and that we needed to make up. He wanted to hug me, he said, to show he had no hard feelings for what I'd done.

"I thought, *If I could shove him out the window, just push him out of my room, get him away.* . . . I said again, 'Please get out.' He went on talking the same way. 'Let's be friends.' And he kept saying my name. 'Patty, Patty . . . let's make up. I want us to be friends.' "

The woman in the apron hung up the phone and came back. "Still here, girls? How're you feeling, young lady?"

"Okay." Patty held out the bottle.

We left the store and walked again. We walked down another steep hill. The sky was so blue.

After a while, Patty started talking again. "My uncle wouldn't leave my room. He sat on the bed and he wouldn't leave. I said, 'Okay, *I'll* leave.' But as soon as I went to the door, he followed me. So I sat down at my desk again and he sat down on the bed again."

"He sounds stupid," I said under my breath. I hated him for doing all that to Patty. Something flashed through my mind, an idea or a picture—a fantasy of me tripping up her uncle, knocking him down, kicking him.

"He started in on me again," she said. " 'Sit on my lap, Patty. Sit on my lap, and we'll make up and forget all this.' I went crazy and started screaming, 'If you don't get out of here, I'm going to call my father!' You know what he said, Sarabeth?

" 'You're going to call Will? Don't you think that I care for you more than Will does? I'm right here, buying the food, paying the rent, buying you clothes, paying your dentist. Call Will, call your father,' he said, 'see how much he cares for you.'

"I screamed, 'Shut up! Shut up!' I ran out of the room. He came after me. I ran, I didn't stop, I can run faster than him, the fat old thing! I ran out of the house. I stayed outside. I walked around the street for a while, and then I hid in the backyard down past the pine trees. It got dark and the lights went on. I saw my uncle come out and walk around the house. He was calling me.

"I didn't answer, and I didn't go in until Mom came home. I saw her drive in. I sneaked into the house. I was lucky—she was in the living room with Uncle Paul. They were talking and they didn't hear me come in."

"Could you hear them? Did he tell her you were gone?"

"I don't know. I bet he didn't. When she came into my room a little later, I was in bed, and I made believe I was asleep. But I didn't sleep all night. I stayed up and I painted. I painted my wall. All night I painted my wall."

"You made more pictures?"

"No! I painted over everything! I smeared it all out."

"Everything?"

"I'm not going home," she said. "I'm never going home again."

The school was below us. We'd walked in a huge circle. "Maybe you could talk to somebody in school," I said. "We could go in now and talk to somebody."

"No. I'm going away. I took my money and I got some money from Mom's room."

I remembered when I went out on the highway and tried to hitchhike. I hadn't wanted to go home then, either. Now I could see that I was lucky that woman had made me go back.

"Patty, why don't you come home with me," I said.

"With you? When?"

"Right now. You can stay with me."

"With you?" She didn't say anything for a minute. Her eyes were unfocused. Then, "Okay," she said on a sigh. She seemed worn-out, as if at that moment she would have gone anywhere that anyone wanted her to.

From a pay phone, I tried calling Cynthia to see if she could pick us up. Mom was at work, there was no point in calling her. But Cynthia wasn't home.

Patty sat down on the sidewalk.

I called Leo. "Leo, it's me, Sarabeth. I need a ride home."

"Aren't you in school?"

"I can't tell you about it now, Leo, but it's important."

"Give me fifteen minutes," he said. "Where are you?"

I told him, then I looked down at Patty, and I said, "I have a friend with me. Would you come for us in the Goldmobile?" I thought that seeing the Goldmobile would make Patty feel better.

We waited for Leo by the phone booth. We didn't say much. Patty seemed all talked out. She was sitting back, her legs out in front of her. When she saw the Goldmobile coming down the street, spiky and flashing and shining, she said, "What's *that?*"

"It's Leo's," I said. I felt proud as I explained about Leo and how he'd bought the old van when he was not much older than we were.

Leo parked next to us. He shook hands with Patty through the window. "Hop in, guys."

"Wait, Leo, I want Patty to look at the Goldmobile." We walked slowly around it. No matter how many times I've seen the Goldmobile, I always find something else to look at, something I missed before or that I want to see again.

I kept pointing out things to Patty: a tragedy

mask, a row of unicorns over the windshield, a circle of foreign coins riveted onto an ashtray shaped like a snapping turtle.

Patty didn't say one word. She had on her public Patty face. I couldn't tell if she liked the Goldmobile or didn't like it, if she was impressed or bored or indifferent.

When we got in the van, she thanked Leo.

"What for?" he said. "Picking you up? Glad to help out."

"I meant for bringing this . . . whatever it is, this beautiful truck of yours. Goldmobile? That's better. It sounds silly to call it a truck. It's not a truck, it's not anything ordinary."

"Oh, do you like it?" All of a sudden, Leo sounded bashful.

"No, I didn't *like* it," she said. "That's not a good enough word."

"Well," Leo said. "Well, okay!"

No questions, nothing about why we weren't in school. He just drove us home.

CHAPTER 27

"*This* is where you live?" Patty said after Leo left us off. "Here? I've passed this trailer park lots of times when we were in the car. I didn't realize you lived here."

She turned her head, looking first one way, then the other, and I began seeing Roadview differently—seeing it and hearing it through Patty's eyes and ears. I'd never noticed the awful, rolling, grinding noise the big semis made out on the highway. The cozy little trailer homes shrank back into a bunch of shabby, peeling shacks on wheels, each with a yard so tiny it would fit easily into Patty's living room. Why had I never realized that Seven's pink awning wasn't cheerful, just tacky? And my magic cliff! It looked menacing, ready to slide down and crush us all without warning.

"Here we are." My heart fell inside my chest. Our trailer looked bare and graceless. I couldn't remember when Mom and I had last washed the windows. One year we'd planted fall flowers in our little yard, bright orange and lavender mums. Why hadn't we thought to do it this year?

"Welcome to Number Two," I said.

"Number Two?"

"It's the second trailer," I said.

"You call it Number *Two?*" she repeated. She half smiled. "That's what babies say when they have to go to the bathroom."

I took out my key. Now she'd see all our old shabby things—the dining room chair with the legs tied with cord and the toaster that only burned the bread. We used paper napkins, our blankets were pilly, and none of our dishes matched. If we needed a cup or a glass, Mom went to a Rescue Mission thrift shop and bought one for a dime.

Tobias came around the side of the house. I looked at him with cold eyes, Patty's eyes. Oh, yes, even he could be better! There was gunk in the corner of his left eye, and one ear was sticky and bloody. "Did you have a fight?" I said. "Tobias, say hello to Patty." He stuck his tail in the air and strolled off.

"Cats always do what they want," I said. There was a hard, sharp feeling in my chest, as if I'd swallowed a chicken bone.

"If I could have another life, I'd come back as a cat," Patty remarked as I struggled with the key.

"Why?" I jiggled the key to the left, to the right, and then to the left again. "Mom fixed this," I muttered, "and it worked for about two days."

"I'd come back as a cat because cats can lead their own lives," Patty said.

The door finally opened, and we went in. "Well, this is the kitchen," I said. "Not very big, is it?" My eyes went to the greenish stain over the stove where pea soup had splattered. "Here's the dining room, I guess you call it the dining room, since there's room enough for a table." I wanted to pull her past the living room and our broken-down couch and faded rose armchair.

I stopped myself. I drew in a breath. I hated this feeling of having to apologize for everything— where I lived and how I lived and what we had. I sat down at the table and pushed out a chair for Patty.

"Talking too much," I said. "Talking too damn much!"

"You don't talk too much," she said.

"I think I just talked your ear off."

"You didn't even come close, Sarabeth. I'm the one who talked *your* ear off, remember?"

"That was different," I said. "I was just blabbing. You were talking about *something.*"

Patty played with the salt and pepper shakers. "Sarabeth, thanks for listening. And thanks for

sticking with me and bringing me home with you."
Her voice was low again.

"No, don't thank me." I reached across the
table for her hand. I felt about *this big*. Patty
hadn't been thinking about our temperamental front
door or our dilapidated furniture.

I heard Tobias at the door, meowing. "I bet he's
been hunting," I said. "He probably has a mouse or
a chipmunk. If we're *really* lucky, he might have
brought us home a rabbit. Yum-yum."

Patty looked up. "Do you eat it?"

"Of course. Rabbit stew. We'll cook it right up,
before Mom gets home."

"I've never eaten it," she said faintly.

"No? How about mouse stew?"

"Mouse—" she began. Then her usually pale
cheeks got bright red. *"Sarabeth!"*

I laughed and let Tobias in. Sure enough, he
had something in his mouth.

"What's he got?" Patty said.

"Don't worry, it's only—" Then I saw what it
was. "It's a rat!"

"A rat!" Patty leaped back.

The rat was alive. Its legs were kicking.

Tobias had the rat clenched between his teeth.
He looked up at me with round warning eyes and
gave a throaty growl. I tried to edge him out the
door, but he wouldn't go. He crouched with the rat.

I knelt down and stroked Tobias. I was careful not to touch the rat. "Patty, open the door," I said. Then, to Tobias, "Good boy, *gooooood* little hunter." His eyes grew smaller. When he was relaxed, I scooped him up and dumped him and the rat outside. Patty slammed the door.

"Want to be a cat now, Patty?" I said.

She gave a little giggle.

"I know this is gross after Tobias and his rat meal, but are you hungry?"

"A little bit."

"Me, too. What'll it be? And don't say a rat sandwich."

We stayed in the rest of the morning. We listened to music for a while. I showed Patty where I kept Mark The Pillow in the closet, and we talked about my "date" with him and his mother. We talked a lot about the other girl. "The mystery girl," I said. "Pamela." I wasn't going to tell Patty about kissing Mark, but then I did.

"Oh, you really love him," she said.

"I know I do. Do you think I'm crazy?"

"No, definitely not." She lay down on my bed. "Right now, I feel good," she said. "Right now, I feel safe. It would be fun to live here. We could be like sisters." She looked around the room. "Where would I sleep? This bed isn't big enough for two of us."

"We have a roll-away cot. Or maybe we could get a bunk bed. I always wanted to sleep on top of a bunk bed."

"What about my clothes?"

"You could share my closet."

"You only have one bureau."

"I'll empty a couple of drawers for you."

"This room is pretty messy."

"Is it?" I looked around. "Are you very neat? Maybe you'll sleep in Mom's room. She's super-neat."

"I'm not superneat, but I'm sort of neat. I guess I could learn to be a little bit sloppy."

I looked around my room again. "I don't think I'm that sloppy."

"Well, you are," Patty said "Look at the stuff on the floor."

"I'll clean it up Saturday," I said. "That's my cleanup day."

"If I was here—if this was my room, too—I'd have to clean it up every day. That's the way I am."

"Really?" I frowned. "I like to wake up early," I said. "What about you?"

"I'm a nightbird. Sometimes I stay up to midnight. Last night I stayed up all night."

"I know. You told me. But that wasn't ordinary. You were so upset and everything."

"Still, it wasn't that hard for me to do."

"Well, maybe you would rather live with Grant or Asa."

Patty leaned up on her elbows. "I'll tell you something, Sarabeth. They've been my best friends forever, but you know what would be neat about living with you? I could be myself. They all have their ideas about me. They've got me in my little slot. Oh, Patty . . . that's the way Patty is . . . Patty has moods . . . Patty this, Patty that . . . You, Sarabeth, don't say that."

"Well . . ." I bent my head, flattered that she thought I was so perceptive.

"You don't even think it," Patty said.

"Oh, Patty, I'm not that good." I had to say it. The truth was I'd probably been worse than anyone about putting Patty into a slot.

Later we got out the cookbooks and read recipes. That made us hungry again and we decided to make brownies. When we took the first batch out of the oven, Patty said, "I suppose we should let them cool."

"Are you crazy, darlink? Vee have to zample theze. If they are no goot, vee don't vant anyone elze to zuffer, eating them, do vee?"

"You're right. It's our duty to try them."

"Be brave, darlink." I ate a brownie. It was soft and sweet. "Zoo? Do you like?"

"Not bad," Patty said. "Let's try one more to be sure."

"You're right, darlink. Vee have a duty to our public. I hope vee can bear up under thizz terrible ztrain."

We wrapped a plateful of brownies in silver paper for Cynthia and delivered them to her house. "Won't she wonder who left them?" Patty asked.

"She'll know it's me, just like I know it's Tobias when I find a mouse on the doorstep."

"Or a rat."

"Let's not talk about that," I said.

We walked over to Mrs. Vander Burgh's trailer, and I rang the bell. She came to the door wearing black-and-white knickers and a big striped shirt. "Hello, Sarabeth. You weren't going to work today, were you?"

"No, I just want to visit Geri, Mrs. Vander Burgh. This is my friend Patty Lewis."

Mrs. Vander Burgh pushed her hair out of her eyes. "No school today, Sarabeth?"

Patty and I looked at each other. "No school for us," I said.

Geri was in her crib, lying on her back, looking up at the ice-cream mobile. "I brought somebody to see you, Geri." She kicked her feet. "That means she's glad for company," I explained.

"She's cute." Patty straightened Geri's little shirt.

When we left, the sky had grayed over and it was raining. I told Patty about Cynthia's being pregnant and how jealous I felt when I first found out.

"I can understand that," Patty said. She pulled up the collar of her jacket. "Geri reminds me of Amanda."

"Who?"

"My father's new little baby."

The way she said it, it took me a moment to realize Amanda was also her sister. "Your sister," I said.

"My half sister."

"How old is she?"

"She's two years old. She's very smart. The first time she saw someone wearing a fur coat, she started petting it. The lady said, 'I bet you'd like one of these when you grow up.' And Amanda said, 'No, fank you'—that's the way she talks—'I have a kitty cat at home.' "

"That's funny."

"I know. My father told me about it. Amanda's all he talks about. If I call him, it's Amanda this, Amanda that. And when I go there, all he wants me to do is baby-sit Amanda or take her to the park or read to her. I guess I really love Amanda, but still, sometimes I get so depressed about her."

The look on Patty's face made me wish I hadn't started this. I remembered Grant saying that Patty felt she didn't even have a father anymore. I took Patty's arm. "Come on, we'll go eat something—"

"Sarabeth, food doesn't fix *everything* up."

"Okay, we'll get my room ready for you to stay."

"Are you sure it's okay? I could leave right now. Maybe I should. I feel I should leave, your mom won't like it that I'm here."

"Patty, it's not so easy to leave this place. No buses. You need a car to get out of here." I saw her glance at the highway. "No, don't think about hitch-hiking. Patty, come on. I know my mom will be glad to have you here."

She still looked so sad and solemn I put my fingers on either side of her mouth and lifted her lips into a smile. "Zmile, darlink, you are maybe my prizoner, but vee treat you goot, I promize!"

CHAPTER 28

Mom was in the shower when we got back. I knocked on the door. "Mom, hi. I have someone home with me."

"Can't hear you," she called. "Wait a sec, I'll be right out."

"Why is she showering now?" Patty said.

"She just came home from work."

"My mother showers in the morning."

"So what?"

"So nothing. Just a comment."

"Dumb comment," I said.

"I guess I'm tense. Sorry."

Mom came out of the shower. She was wearing a towel around her head, her blue bathrobe, and slippers. Patty had only seen Mom from a distance, in the car, when she came to pick me up after the party.

"This is Patty," I said. Patty and Mom shook hands. Then Mom went into her room and I started getting things ready for supper. "You want to do the napkins?" I showed Patty how we folded them like birds with their wings tucked back.

"Your mom is tiny," Patty said.

"She's four feet eleven."

"She looks more like a sister than a mother."

"Well, I guess she's not very old. She had me when she was sixteen."

Patty's eyes widened. "Sixteen? That's so young! I thought—" She broke off.

"What'd you think?"

"Nothing."

"It's really irritating when people start to say something and don't finish."

Patty shrugged. "I thought only messed-up kids had babies so young."

"My mom's not messed up," I said coldly.

"I know, I can see that. That's why I didn't want to say it, Silver."

She said my name very nicely. Every time someone called me Silver, I felt soft toward them. I liked that name a lot better than Sarabeth. "Patty—Grant and I were thinking about talking to Mrs. Packwood about you and—you know— your uncle."

"The librarian? You told her? Why did you tell her?"

"Patty, we didn't say anything to her, don't worry! But what if we did? *You* haven't done anything wrong."

"I don't want it spread all over the world, Sarabeth."

While we were eating supper, Mom asked what time Patty's mother was coming to pick her up.

Patty glanced at me.

"Patty's going to stay overnight, Mom. Tonight—and a few more nights, too. We'll get out the roll-away. She's going to stay with us for a while."

"For a *while?*" Mom's eyebrows went up. "Until when?"

"Well . . . until she wants to go home."

"Really?"

"I told her you wouldn't mind if she stayed with us. She's got problems at home."

"What kind of problems?"

"I don't think Patty wants to talk about them."

"But maybe she'd better, Sarabeth. Because you can't just ask to stay at someone's house indefinitely. I mean, what's the reason?"

"It's a good reason, Mom. Can't you trust me?"

"I don't see what trust has to do with it. I should have some idea of what's going on if someone is coming into my house like this."

"Mom! I never thought you would be this way. I promised Patty she could stay here."

"Well, maybe you should have asked me first."

"Why? It's my home, too!"

"And who pays the bills?" Mom said. "Don't get above yourself, Sarabeth."

"Maybe you'd like it better if we both left!"

"That's hardly necessary. Why don't you just tell me what's going on?"

"No!"

"Sarabeth." Patty was looking really unhappy. "I'll tell your mom. It's okay."

"You said you didn't want to tell!"

"I changed my mind."

I threw down my napkin. "Isn't anybody consistent in this world?"

"No," Mom said, "and you might as well learn it right now, hon."

I stamped out of the room and down the hall. Let Patty tell my mother whatever she wanted to. Phooey! I thought. Phooey! The way Mom played Big Boss really got under my skin. I slammed the bathroom door a couple of times. Then I went back to the table.

Patty was telling Mom about her uncle.

"There's one thing I don't understand," Mom said, "why your mother doesn't believe you."

Patty put her face in her hands. "I'm not going to stay here," she muttered.

"Mom, what's the matter with you?" I could hardly control myself. How could she say that in front of Patty? I always thought Mom was careful about people's feelings. "What if I told you someone was doing this stuff to me? Would you believe me?"

"I would."

"What if it was somebody you really liked doing it to me? What if it was Leo?"

Mom looked shocked. "He wouldn't. Leo wouldn't do a thing like that. I know Leo."

"That's what Patty's mother says. She says it's her brother and she knows him."

Patty looked up. She was drawing her lips in and sucking on them nervously.

"It doesn't *show* on her uncle, Mom. You couldn't tell from looking at him. He doesn't look weird or act weird. He doesn't have fangs. He's nice, he's polite, he's generous, isn't he, Patty? He drove me home."

"What do you mean he drove you home?" Mom said.

"From the concert. I told you."

"That was Patty's uncle?"

"Yes."

"And you knew—"

"Oh!" I said. "Now you're singing a different tune, Mom. Now it's me, and you're worried."

Mom flushed and didn't say anything for a moment.

Patty was just sitting there, looking at the wall and sucking on her lips.

"Patty"—I touched her hand—"Patty, it's going to be okay."

She didn't move. Tears came to her eyes.

"Oh, hon!" Mom got her arms around Patty and pulled her onto her lap. I almost laughed. Patty was twice as big as Mom. "You can stay," Mom said. "You stay as long as you want to . . . but does your mother have any idea where you are?"

Patty shook her head.

"She's probably pretty upset by now. Let me call her and tell her you're here. Okay?"

While Mom phoned Mrs. Lewis, Patty and I went into my room. I gave her my green monogrammed pajamas. We both changed. I turned on the radio. We did everything as if it was an ordinary evening. But of course it wasn't.

CHAPTER 29

Patty and I were in my room when Mom called, "Your mother's here, Patty."

"What am I going to do?" Patty said. "My mother'll make me go home."

"No, you're staying here."

"You don't know my mother, Sarabeth. She's the kind of person you can't argue with. She's always reasonable. She always has something else to say, another argument, another point." Patty went to the window, then she came back to the bed and sat down. "She always wins."

"Patty, if your mom makes you go home, I'll just have to go, too, and live with you."

She was shivering, and I gave her my red bathrobe.

"Are you girls coming?" Mom called.

I put my arm through Patty's, and we went into the living room. Mrs. Lewis was standing by the window. She was wearing a belted raincoat and a rain hat with a wide brim. "Patty!" she said. "You had me worried sick. I called Grant, Asa . . . no one knew where you were."

"I'm not going home with you," Patty said.

"Of course you are. Get dressed."

"I'm not going home."

"Patty, we can talk at—"

"We can't talk! You don't listen to me! I told you what Uncle Paul is doing, and *you don't listen to me.*"

"I do. I think you're dis—"

"I'm not disturbed," Patty shouted. "Why won't you believe me? I'm not crazy! I'm telling the truth."

Mrs. Lewis had two big red spots on her cheeks. So did Patty. She looked feverish, as if she should be in bed with blankets up to her chin.

"Why don't you believe Patty?" I said to Mrs. Lewis.

"Sarabeth, stay out of this," Mom said.

Mrs. Lewis turned to Mom. "I'm ashamed that Patty and I are carrying on like this in front of strangers. I don't know what you can think of us. It seems you know everything Patty has been saying

about my brother. This whole thing is terribly upsetting. My brother is just not the kind of person—"
She broke off and tightened the belt on her raincoat. "Patty, will you please get dressed. You look exhausted. I know I'm exhausted."

"I'm staying here."

"Patty, you have a home."

"It's not my home. It's *his*. I hate it. I'll never live there again. Do you hear me? Never! You believe him."

"He's my brother—"

"I'm your daughter," Patty said. "I'm your *daughter*. What about me?"

Mrs. Lewis tried to put her arm around Patty's shoulder. Until that moment, everyone had been more or less calm. Then everything exploded. Patty ran to the phone and started screaming that she was going to call her father and the newspapers and the TV stations. "I'll tell them who Uncle Paul is. I'll tell them what he did. I'll tell everyone! I don't care!"

Mrs. Lewis yanked Patty away from the phone. "Stop! You're hysterical." She started dragging her toward the door. Patty clung to the sofa.

"We're going home," Mrs. Lewis said. "You're coming home with me."

"I'm not. *I'm not!*"

My heart started going *whomp, whomp, whomp* in my chest. "Let her go," I said.

Patty wrenched free and ran into my room. I ran after her.

"Close the door! Keep her out!" Patty was breathing hard. She went inside the closet and slammed the door on herself. Then she came bursting out. "No! I can't!"

Patty's mother opened the door to my room. "Don't come in," I said. "This is my room."

"Keep out, keep out," Patty cried.

Then, in what seemed like an instant, Patty threw herself across the room, pushed up the window, and flung herself out.

The wet darkness. The red of the bathrobe, trailing behind. And then a cry. And the crash of her body hitting the ground.

And another cry, a long, wailing cry. "Patty! Patty!" It was her mother.

CHAPTER 30

Her mother's cry.

The open window.

Patty's scream.

Rain.

All of that is in my memory, but silent, quiet, like a black-and-white photograph.

That's the first picture—my room and Patty out the window. The next picture, the next thing I remember, is crowding and rushing through the kitchen door, Tobias underfoot, and Mom saying, "Don't go out in your pajamas." Even then, in the rush and fear, I remember thinking that was silly. And later, Mom couldn't believe she'd said that.

I guess we all had the same thought—getting to Patty. Did I say we crowded through the door together? Wrong. There was no "crowd" at the door, only Mom and me. Mrs. Lewis went out the window after Patty. That big woman out that little window.

By the time Mom and I came around the side of the trailer, she was already there with Patty, kneeling on the ground, cradling Patty in her arms.

The light from my room shone down. And yet it was dark, and the cliff behind us was dark and lumpy, a dark, looming shape in the rain.

"I'm sorry," Mrs. Lewis was saying. "Oh, Patty, I'm sorry . . . so sorry . . ." She was crying, and Patty was crying, too.

The rain drummed on the trailer roof. My heart was doing that *whomp, whomp, whomp* kind of thing, only I wasn't frightened now. And then I heard Tobias giving one of his funny *meow*s. He came around the side of the trailer, his tail drooping, his fur wet and flattened. He climbed into Patty's lap, licked her hand for a moment, and then turned and began cleaning his face.

"Well, Tobias," Patty said in a shaky voice, "you think I sat down here for your pleasure?"

Mrs. Lewis stood up then, and Patty did, too, or tried to. Something was wrong with her right foot. She couldn't put her weight on it.

We drove to the emergency room of St. Lucy's Hospital. We sat on wooden chairs in the hall near the nurses' station. Patty and her mother held hands. Something had changed between them. I could feel it, the way you feel the air is different after a thunderstorm—clearer, lighter, cleaner.

"Patty Lewis?" The doctor came out. "I'm Doctor Legasy. In here, please."

We all went in with Patty and watched while the doctor examined her. A small bone in her foot was broken, but the cast the doctor put on went up to her knee. When the doctor was finished, she started filling out a form, asking Patty where and how the accident happened.

"I jumped out a window."

"Did you slip on a rug or something like that? Should I put down a domestic accident?" She yawned. She had small, tired blue eyes.

"No," Patty said. "I jumped out a window."

"Oh, dear." The doctor gave Mrs. Lewis a sympathetic look, as if to say Patty was probably a handful. "Nasty little break, but it'll mend fine," she said.

We drove back to our house. Mom put on water to heat, and we sat around the table, drinking hot tea and eating the rest of the brownies.

Mrs. Lewis was writing in a little leather notebook. "We'll have to move. There's a dozen things I have to think about—somewhere to live, a job. What'll I do about school?" She lifted her teacup in both hands. "You girls made these brownies?

They're good." She gave me a wan smile.

She and Mom agreed that Patty would stay with us for a few days, at least until Mrs. Lewis could, as she said, "get things straightened out." We talked about practical stuff, like how much clothing Patty would need and if Mrs. Lewis would bring it over here or Mom would pick it up.

"I appreciate this," Mrs. Lewis said. "I can't tell you—"

"No, it's fine," Mom said, "as long as the girls don't mind sharing a room—"

"We don't mind," Patty and I said, almost together.

CHAPTER 31

Maybe I shouldn't have been so quick to say I wanted Patty to stay with me. The first week she never stopped complaining well, not complaining so much as comparing everything about the way we lived to the way she was used to living. It started the first morning when we had to get up to go to school.

"I don't get up this early."

"We have to catch the bus, Patty."

She huddled under the covers. "It's still dark out."

"The days are getting shorter, but, like Mom says, look on the cheerful side. December twenty-first the days start getting longer. Winter solstice."

"Shut up," Patty said.

I finished getting dressed. "You want the bathroom first?"

"We have to take turns?"

"You want to go outdoors?"

"Okay! Okay! You know I'm not at my greatest when an alarm wakes me up. And I can't stand being talked to in the morning. Mom knows that and she doesn't bug me."

"Okay!" Was I bugging her?

On the bus, Patty didn't say much. She sat next to the window with her cool, superior face. Did she want to make sure everyone knew she wasn't a real bus kid?

It didn't help matters any when she said how filthy the bus floor was. The floor *was* muddy, but it was the way she said it, as if it were something I was personally responsible for.

At lunch, Patty and I filled Asa, Jennifer, and Grant in on everything that had happened.

"You jumped out the *window?*" Jennifer said. She was smiling. "I never thought you had that kind of guts, Patty."

"It wasn't guts, Jennifer. I didn't even know I was doing it. The whole thing was like a dream."

"A nightmare?" I said.

"Yes . . . that's a better word." Patty had her injured foot propped up on the bench so we could all sign the cast.

"What I can't get over is your uncle," Asa said.

"I mean, that's as if someone like my father—"

"Listen," Jennifer said, "I've read about this stuff. It doesn't matter if the man is a judge or a janitor. I mean, all kinds of men do this. You wouldn't believe! *All* kinds, and they all make me want to puke!"

Grant had been silent. "I kept wondering where you two were yesterday." She gave me a little frown. "I wondered if you were skipping school."

"We didn't set out to do that," I said. "That wasn't exactly the point."

"I *do* understand that, Sarabeth."

I looked at her in surprise. Was she miffed that all these things had happened to Patty with *me* and not her? I tried to downplay what I'd done for Patty. I didn't want Grant to think I was pushing in between her and Patty. Yet there was one part of me that liked the attention, that liked being in the center of all this excitement.

"It really was lucky for me Sarabeth found me," Patty said again. "I don't know where I'd be right now if she hadn't come along."

Grant was writing her name in colored ink on Patty's cast. "You might be walking around on two feet instead of hobbling around in this thing."

Sunday afternoon Patty and I went shopping at the mall. Mom told me to buy myself some socks and then take Patty to a movie. "My treat."

"Mom, can we afford—"

"Shhh, don't argue with me, Sarabeth."

Almost the first person I saw when we walked into the mall was Mark. He was sitting between two adults behind a long table that had been set up near the pizza shop. A big red-lettered sign draped across the bottom of the table read HELP SAVE ENDANGERED WILDLIFE. S.A.M.E. (SAVE MOTHER EARTH).

"Isn't that Mark Emelsky?" Patty said.

We walked toward the table. Mark pushed his glasses up on his nose and smiled. "Hi, Sarabeth. Oh, it's Patty, too."

"We came over to see what you're doing," I said. I felt dizzy just looking at him.

"We're asking the state legislature for more money for endangered species and to make sure natural habitats aren't destroyed. Do you know we almost lost bluebirds? I mean *bluebirds!* When we lose a bird, we can never get it back again." He held out a pencil. "You'll sign, won't you?"

"Don't you want just voters?" I asked.

"No, we want everyone," the woman said. She was wearing a red shirt with S.A.M.E. written on the pocket. "Put your age down. You're going to be voting in a few years."

I bent over and signed the sheet. I jostled Patty's arm. "Sign, Patty," I ordered. Maybe I was showing off a little for Mark. Patty took the pencil and scrawled her name.

"Well, I guess we should go," I said. But I was hoping Mark would say, *Oh, no. Hang around awhile, Sarabeth. When am I going to see you again? I've really missed you.*

"See you around," he said, and he winked at me.

A wink? What was a wink? How did a wink compare with a kiss? Had he forgotten? He could at least have said something personal. Bluebirds! That was all we'd talked about. Even a special look would have been better than that wink.

"Same old Mark," Patty said, as we walked away. "Still in training to be St. Francis." She went into the cheese and coffee shop. "I want to buy something for your mom." We went around the counter, sampling the cheeses. Patty ordered half a pound of Brie.

I looked at the price. "Patty, that's too expensive." She handed me a sample on a little cracker. It was soft, creamy, and sharp. "It almost tastes like custard."

"That's exactly how it's supposed to taste," Patty said. "You have to know about cheeses, Sarabeth, if you're going to be a chef." I'd noticed Patty liked to tell me things, lecture me, teach me.

"Do you know what these are?" she said, pointing to a basket of strange-looking fruit, like bumpy green pineapples, on the floor near the cash register. "They're breadfruit."

A dark-skinned man in a business suit heard her. "Ah, breadfruit. It's tropical, wonderful. You never ate breadfruit, young ladies? You are truly missing something." He had a West Indian accent. "To prepare, you peel the breadfruit," he said. "You slice it and roast it and oh, mon!" He laughed and touched his fingers to his mouth. "As the people say, it's lick-your-finger good, mon!" He smiled at me. "Angels have made the breadfruit."

"I'm going to buy one," I said. I thought of Mark. Maybe I would roast the breadfruit and ask him over to share it with us. "I want to try every kind of food in the world," I said. The man made breadfruit sound so wonderful, I didn't even ask how much it cost.

Asa, Jennifer, Patty, and I went over to Grant's house one day after school. Mom was working in the neighborhood and was going to pick Patty and me up later. We fooled around, making malteds in the kitchen, and then we went up to Grant's room and ended up having a pillow fight, with Asa trying to catch the action on Grant's stepfather's video camera.

Later, we started talking about Patty's uncle

again and how nothing had happened to him. "I just want to forget him," Patty said.

"You can't just forget," Asa said.

"Yes, I can."

"Patty, you can't act like it never happened. Something should be done about your uncle."

"Like, your mother ought to to have him slammed in the hoosegow," Jennifer said with one of her cackles. "Or make him walk around with a sign around his neck. DANGER. STAY AWAY FROM ME."

"That's a little bizarre," Asa said. "But he committed a crime and he should be punished."

Patty started sucking in her lips, that nervous gesture of hers. "Asa, you want to spread it all over? You want it to be in the newspapers what he did to me? You want everyone to know, everything to be public and ugly?"

"What if he does it to some other girl?"

"Oh," Patty breathed.

"It was you now," Asa said. "But who knows?"

Patty was getting more and more agitated.

"Asa," I said, "your father has lunch with Patty's uncle every week. What are you going to do about that? Do you think that's right? Do you think your father ought to be eating lunch with someone like Patty's uncle?"

Asa slumped down on the bed. "You're right,

Silver." She looked stricken. "Patty, I'm going to tell my father."

"No!" Patty said. "No. No, no, no. I just want to stop talking about my uncle! I just want to forget him."

CHAPTER 32

Patty stayed with Mom and me for almost a month while Mrs. Lewis found a job and a place to live. A month is a long time.

For a while, Patty and I did everything together. She even went along with me on Saturdays when I worked at Mrs. Vander Burgh's. She took care of Geri while I cleaned. At first she didn't want to take money from Mrs. Vander Burgh.

"That's not real work," she said, "not like what you do, Silver. It's easy playing with the baby. Anyway, you can tell she doesn't have much money. I mean, everything in their place, all their furniture and stuff, is sort of cheap, isn't it?"

I didn't answer. I'd never noticed that the Vander Burghs' stuff was that much different from what we had. If anything, it was better.

Patty gave a kind of shudder. "I wonder if that's what Mom and I'll have, now that we're going to be poor, too."

I didn't say anything to that, either.

One day I called Mark at Patty's suggestion. "Get things cleared up," Patty said. "Ask him what his intentions are."

"I can't do that!"

"Well, find out more about the girl with the white eyebrows. I think it's Pamela Schooner. Her brother Tim is in the class behind us."

I went to the phone, and then I hesitated. "Are you sure I should do this?"

"How long can you have a romance with a pillow?" she said.

Mark's sister Katie answered the phone. "Mark's not home. You want to leave a message?"

"Yes," Patty hissed in my ear.

"Tell him Sarabeth called."

"Will do."

"Still playing basketball, Katie?"

"Who's this?" she said.

"It's Sarabeth!" Who did she think it was, King Kong?

"How do you know I play basketball?"

That crushed me. Did the whole family have a case of amnesia?

* * *

Patty and I would get along fine for a few days, and then suddenly things would flare up between us and we'd be fighting. If Mom was home, she cut it right off. "Button up, you girls. This place is too small for that! I'm not listening to that stuff after I've worked my butt off all day."

So I'd take a walk, or Patty would, but it frustrated her that there was no place to really *go*. "You can walk around Roadview in five minutes," she fumed. "Then what do you do? Climb the cliff? Commit suicide on the highway?"

During the day, if we weren't getting along, we could more or less stay out of each other's way. But at night, even when we were fighting, we had to crowd into my room together. Then the silence could be awfully loud.

I blamed Patty for our fights. She could be withdrawn, cold, snobby. And she had a mouth on her. Among other things, she called me picky and oversensitive. I'd lie in bed and think, *Why do I have to live with someone who feels that way about me? Why does everything I do now have to be done with someone else?*

Even a simple thing like watching TV with Mom wasn't my private treat anymore. Patty was there, lying on the other side of Mom, making her sophisticated comments, making Mom laugh. Sometimes I laughed, too, and sometimes I even liked the three of us being together. It was cozy and fun. But plenty of times, I felt resentful and uncomfortable. I wasn't used to feeling that way. I wasn't used to sharing things. So, maybe I was finding out things about Patty's nature that I didn't like, but I was also finding out things about my own nature that weren't all that pleasant.

If there were days when I wished with all my heart that Patty's mom would hurry up about finding that place for them to live, there were also other days, and plenty of them, when I never wanted her to leave. "Do you think this is what sisters are like?" I said.

Patty shrugged. "How would I know?" That was the way she could dump cold water on me. Then I felt she was just tolerating living with me.

But you could never tell with Patty. The very next day in school, Grant asked Patty to come live with her. "You're always saying how crowded you are at Silver's," Grant said. "Why don't you just move over to my house? You could have your own room and bathroom, no problem."

Patty shook her head. "I'm staying at Silver's, that's where I want to be." She pressed her foot against mine under the table. Above the table, she gave one of her indifferent shrugs.

And all at once I understood something about Patty. All those careless shrugs and jaded, bored looks were her way of protecting herself. She kept people off with them. She made you feel that she had a big NO TRESPASSING sign posted. But the real Patty—and I knew it by now—was not so detached. She was wounded. People—grown-ups—had hurt her, and she was making sure no one else did.

When Jennifer's pajama party came around in October, my mother drove the two of us over. Patty's mother was going to drive us back in the morning.

I couldn't help remembering the first pajama party at Patty's house, how I'd almost not gone at all and how far apart Patty and I had been then. Now we were close, closer even than I'd been to Grant, closer than I'd ever been to another girl.

But at the pajama party we almost had a big fight. In fact, all five of us had a big fight. It was about Patty's uncle again.

I was the one who started it this time. I had been thinking that if what happened to Patty had happened to me and nobody did anything about it, I would want to kill someone. And I said it. "I really mean that. When I think of him, I want to kill Patty's uncle. I wish somebody would."

"That's uncivilized," Asa said. "We don't do things that way in this country. We have a justice system."

I even shocked Jennifer. "Who would've thought Sarabeth would be so vicious?"

"Besides, Sarabeth, did you ever think that maybe Mr. Dexter just needs therapy?" Grant said. "I mean, he is normal in every other way, isn't he, Patty?"

Patty frowned. "I suppose so. My mother's going to warn him. I talked to her on the phone last night. She's going to tell him she'll be keeping her eye on him from now on."

"Keeping her *eye* on him?" Asa said. "What does that mean?"

Patty laughed nervously. "So he doesn't bother anyone else."

"*Bother* anyone? Is that what he did to you, Patty? *Bothered* you?"

"Asa! You know what I'm saying."

"And you know what *I'm* trying to say. I'm trying to get something across to you, Patty."

"Leave Patty alone," Grant said. She moved closer to Patty.

Asa cast her eyes up to the ceiling. "Patty doesn't need you to defend her, Grant. All I'm saying is that I think Patty's mother warning her uncle is ridiculous. It's like a slap on the wrist. Big deal! Boo hoo! He's getting off scot-free."

"What do you want her to do?" Grant said. "Put him in jail?"

"Yes. That's the idea. Now you've got it."

Patty's left eye twitched. "Asa, as long as he doesn't do anything to anyone else, does it matter?"

"Yes! Why should he get away with it? I don't believe in two standards of justice. I tell you, when I'm a lawyer, I'm not going to help people like that get away with things."

"You're concerned with justice," Patty said, "but I don't care about justice. I just want to be left alone."

"That's damn selfish," Asa said.

"Oh, Asa, I'm bored already from your talk," Jennifer said.

"Shut up, Jen," Asa said.

"Why don't you all shut up?" Grant said. "Patty doesn't want to talk about it."

"No, Grant, I want to say one more thing," Patty said. "And then *all* of you can just shut up about it! He's *my* uncle, not yours. And I don't want to be the one to put him in jail."

"Why not? Why *not*?" Asa asked. She was like a little dog nipping at Patty's heels.

"If it was your father—would you do it?"

"It wasn't my father."

We all started shouting at once.

"Would you?" Patty demanded. "Would you put your father in jail, someone from your own family?"

"Yes," Asa said finally. "If he did something like that, yes, I would."

One Saturday, Mom, Leo, and I helped Patty and Mrs. Lewis move. We were at the yellow house on Shadow Lane Road early in the morning. Patty's uncle was gone for the day. We carried everything down the back stairs and out through the kitchen and loaded Leo's truck.

Mrs. Lewis had found an apartment with two bedrooms. "They're tiny," she told Mom as we drove over. "But that's what took me so long. I wanted those two bedrooms so Patty could have some privacy. And I had to find something I could afford, which was nearly impossible because I can't afford much of anything."

"Sounds familiar," Mom said.

At the new apartment, we unloaded the truck and carried everything up the stairs. "My bedroom is even smaller than yours!" Patty said. It had a slanted ceiling and old faded wallpaper with fat yellow roses. "I can always paint over them," she said.

"Don't you like yellow roses? I think they're beautiful."

"Oh well . . . maybe I'll keep them, for you. So you can see them when you visit me."

We worked most of the day, getting everything into place. "I just can't thank you enough," Mrs. Lewis said at least ten times. "I never thought strangers—no, I shouldn't say that. You're not strangers anymore." She hugged Mom and me, and Leo, too.

"Leo's so funny-looking," Patty said later, when we took a walk around her new neighborhood. "I always want to laugh when I see him. He's got those shoulders out to here and then those skinny legs."

It was exactly what I'd thought plenty of times, but I got offended when Patty said it. "I think Leo is extremely good-looking."

"His face is, but his body is weird," Patty said in her flat, sophisticated voice.

"You're so critical," I started to say, then I stopped. I knew Patty pretty well by now and I could tell that she was tense because of the move. It didn't mean I liked what she said about Leo, but at least I didn't blow it up into a big fight.

It was strange that night to have my room to myself again. We hadn't moved the roll-away cot out yet, or even folded it up. Even so, the room felt huge. And it was so quiet in the trailer. I couldn't get used to it. I thought Tobias was looking for Patty, too. He kept coming in and sniffing the cot.

Not too long after Patty moved, two things happened.

First, Patty told us she was going to start seeing a therapist. "I think I hate my uncle so much that it's been twisting me," she said. "You guys going to think I'm crazy now?"

"Are you kidding, Patty?" Asa said. "Don't you know my father went to therapy last year? And he's definitely not crazy."

"Why'd he go to therapy?" I asked.

"He needed it. Something happened in his life that he needed to talk about and get some help on."

"A *judge?*"

Asa gave me the bread-box look. "Silver, that's just his job. He's a person, isn't he?"

"What do you do in therapy? Talk, or what?"

"A lot of talk," Asa said as if she knew everything about it. "Mostly talk about your problems and how you're going to handle them."

"Mom's going to do it, too," Patty said, "because she's got a lot of guilt feelings. And me—I think I should do it because sometimes my mind feels really bad."

"Who's going to pay for it?" I asked.

Jennifer laughed. "Leave it to Silver to ask the practical."

"Mom says we can get family therapy from the county."

"Maybe you should get your uncle to pay. Like reparations," Asa suggested.

"What's that?" I asked. I braced myself for the bread-box look again.

"Reparations are payments for when you've been wronged in a terrible way. My father told me some survivors of the Holocaust got reparations after the war. It wasn't much. It was symbolic, mostly."

I nodded. Was I ever going to know as much as Asa and the others did? Sometimes I thought I should just stop asking questions, but then I'd never know anything, would I?

The second thing that happened I found out about from a newspaper article that Mom put up on the refrigerator under a magnet. The headline said DA PROBES BANKER INVOLVEMENT IN SEX ABUSE. The article didn't give any names, just talked about a "prominent local banker" being investigated on charges of abuse of a minor.

I called Grant. "Did you see in the newspaper about Patty's uncle?"

"No. What?"

I read her the article.

"Oh, I'm glad," she said.

"Me, too. Do you think Patty told? Or her mother?"

"I suppose so. I'm going to call her and find out."

"Call me back," I said. But it was Asa who called me.

"Silver? I was just talking to Grant. She said you wanted to know about Patty's uncle. . . . Well,

I'm the one." Asa sounded a little defiant. "I told my father. I didn't know I was going to do it. We went skiing together last week in Vermont—"

"I remember you said something about it—"

"—And, well, I just started telling him about Patty."

"Did he believe you?"

"Yes."

"I mean, right away?"

"He was pretty upset. He's a friend of Patty's uncle. He said he'd have somebody check up on it, that he couldn't do anything himself—"

We were both quiet for a moment. Then I said, "Does he still have Tuesday lunch with Patty's uncle?"

"Silver, I never met anybody who could think of so many questions!"

"Well, does he?"

"I don't know!"

"Find out," I said, "but don't tell me unless the answer is *no!*"

CHAPTER 33

Billy and Cynthia kissed again and gazed into each other's eyes. "I see Leo watching us," Billy said. "What is it, man? Jealous?"

"Damn straight," Leo said.

We were all eating dinner out at a Mexican restaurant on Route 11. Billy had ordered burritos, enchiladas, guacamole, and I don't know what else. We had just about everything on the menu. My favorite were the tostados. They looked like big bright-yellow seashells and they were delicious.

The evening was Billy and Cynthia's treat, to celebrate their eighteenth wedding anniversary. We were all dressed up and festive. I had my hair braided in five or six braids, the way I'd seen Grant wearing her hair in the supermarket, and my blouse was new—cream-colored linen with embroidery around the neck, a present from Patty and Mrs. Lewis. Leo had embroidery, too, on his vest. His hair was slicked back and he wore a pearl earring in his right earlobe.

"Boy, we are all so gorgeous," Mom said. She smoothed her blue satin skirt. She wore matching blue spike heels, which she said killed her feet. *"But they give me two more inches, so it's worth it."*

Billy and Cynthia attracted the most attention from people. First, because the restaurant manager unfurled a glittery silver banner over our table. *H*A*P*P*Y*   *A*N*N*I*V*E*R*S*A*R*Y*. Mom had tipped him off. Second, because of the way they looked. Billy was in his full uniform. Cynthia wore a pink silk shirt with BABY spelled out in rhinestones and a rhinestone arrow pointing to her belly.

"You're getting so huge," I said.

"What do you expect from an almost-seven-month-pregnant lady?"

"Oh, I can't wait for that baby," Mom said.

"You could have one of your own," Leo said. "The offer's still good."

Everyone laughed. Billy had ordered wine with the meal and they were all in a great mood. I was, too, until Cynthia sprang her news. "Billy and I are house hunting."

"What?" I said. "You're doing what?"

"We're looking for a house to buy, Sarabeth. Isn't that exciting?"

"You're going to leave Roadview?" I was shocked. Roadview without Cynthia and Billy? Me without Cynthia?

"Well, I wouldn't put it that way. It's not going to happen that fast. *If* we find something we like, *if* we can afford it, and *if* the bank will give us a loan, then we'll probably do it."

I must have made some kind of funny noise. Cynthia put her hand over mine. "Hey, sweetie, take it easy."

"Why? Why are you leaving?" My eyes started to smart.

"We can't bring up a kid in that tiny place, Sarabeth."

"Move into another trailer. You can have ours, it's got two bedrooms."

"And what will you and Jane do?"

"We'll switch with you. We don't care, do we, Mom?"

"We probably won't find anything for ages, Sarabeth," Cynthia said.

"What do you need a house for, anyway?"

Billy reached across the table. "Take it easy, kiddo, it's not the end of the world." He touched me on the nose.

I jerked away. I didn't want to be comforted and treated like a child. They were leaving. I could see it on their faces. They were talking about *if* they found a house, but they were going to go.

Later I lay awake for a long time in bed, thinking about all the things that had happened since school began. I was working, I had friends, I'd been involved in something important and serious with Patty, I'd met Mark—and now Cynthia was moving.

Questions came into my mind about Cynthia, and then about Patty and Mark and Grant. And more questions about Patty's uncle, and Mom and Leo, and Cynthia's baby. I felt dizzy thinking about all these things. My world had always been safe, and I had known everything about it. Was everything changing? It had changed already. I sat up and turned on the light. I looked all around the room. Tobias was on the windowsill. Seeing me awake, he sat up.

"Get on my feet," I commanded. "They're cold." As if he understood, he did it. He curled up on my feet. For some reason that calmed me, and I went to sleep.

In January, when we went back to school after the winter vacation, Grant and Patty joined the Drama Club. Almost every day they had noon-hour meetings or rehearsals, so the five of us didn't get to eat lunch together too much.

Then Asa got a boyfriend—someone from Grant's and my homeroom actually, Richard Adamski, a big, shy guy—and she started eating lunch with him. So it was just Jennifer and me. It was fun being with Jennifer. She talked, she always had a story to tell, something to say. She was the one who showed me the article in the newspaper about Patty's uncle.

The headline this time was BANKER CHARGED IN ABUSE CASE. The article stated, "A prominent local banker, Paul Dexter, has been charged . . ." Lower in the article, it said, "The name of the child will not be revealed because she is under age. Margie Hennissey, assistant district attorney, who is prosecuting the case, is confident that . . ."

"And Patty never said a word." Jennifer's eyes snapped. "She is so secretive. That's one thing I like about you, Silver, you don't keep things to yourself."

"In other words, I'm a blabbermouth."

"That's one way of putting it," Jennifer agreed.

"But it must be hard for Patty," I said, "like going through it all again."

"Yeah," Jennifer said. "I think you're right."

When I saw Patty, I started to say something about her uncle, but she cut me off. She was distant. She seemed to be the Patty I first knew: cool, aloof.

If I hadn't been through so much with her, I would never have known there was more to her than what she showed the world. It was as if there was another Patty inside her, a hidden Patty, like the present Leo brought Mom for her birthday, a papier-mâché rabbit. Take off the top of the rabbit and there is another rabbit inside, take off the top of that rabbit and there is still another one inside that . . . Mom loved it. She kept it on her bureau. Sometimes I went in her room and opened it up and took out the rabbits and lined them up. There were five of them altogether, each smaller than the next but each perfectly made.

CHAPTER 34

Over the weekend, Leo took Mom and me to a movie. The minute we walked into the lobby, I saw Mark and Pamela, the girl with the white eyebrows. The lobby was mobbed, but my eyes zoomed right to the two of them. Mark saw me, too.

"Hi, Sarabeth," he said.

And I said, "Hi, Mark The Pillow."

I said it! Right out loud. "Hi, Mark The Pillow."

For one minute, I hoped I hadn't said it. Or that he hadn't heard me.

I'd said it.

And he'd heard me.

Hi, Mark The Pillow.

He stared at me, and then he blushed. Oh, how

he blushed! He got red spots on his cheekbones, and his forehead got red, and his ears were bright red. He blushed as if he knew why I'd said it. And then he looked at Pamela with the white eyebrows in a way that told me everything.

He looked at her, and I thought, *Oh!* Just that. *Oh!*

And I knew—one of those things you know without knowing *how* you know, but you do—that Mark didn't just like her, he liked her a lot, a whole lot, a whole lot better, *much better,* than he liked me.

"Coming?" Leo said. He held up the tickets.

I went in with him and Mom. We took our seats. A minute later, Mark and Pamela took seats just two rows in front of us. I had a perfect view of them. Did Mark do that on purpose? To torture me?

I couldn't concentrate on the movie. I had no idea what was going on. When it was over—at last— I wanted to get out of there, but Mom and Leo dawdled, trying to decide if they should go dancing. Mom had to work the next day. "We won't stay late," Leo said. "Come on, Janie." He raised his hands and snapped his fingers over his head.

Then Mark and Pamela, one pair of glittering glasses and shining braces, one set of angelic eyebrows, walked up the aisle. She had her hand on his shoulder. I wanted to hide, dive under the seat, disappear. Instead, I gazed into space and smiled dreamily, as if I was thinking of something so wonderful I couldn't be bothered to notice the ordinary world and ordinary people with glasses and white eyebrows.

We drove home. Mom and Leo had decided to go dancing, but Mom wanted to change her shoes. "Sure you're going to be all right, hon?"

"Yes. I'm fine. Go ahead. Have a good time." I wanted to be alone so I could be totally miserable. As soon as they were gone, I took a shower and washed my hair. I always wash my hair when I'm feeling awful.

Then, in my room, for the first time in a long time, I took Mark The Pillow out of the closet. I didn't look at him. I just held him against me and felt sad. "I thought you liked me as much as I liked you," I said.

I sat down on the bed. I let Mark The Pillow sit on my lap. I thought about Mark kissing Pamela, kissing her white eyebrows. And I cried a little. Tobias meowed around my legs, trying to comfort me, but Mark The Pillow only gazed up at me. His red face looked smug. His eyes were open and untroubled.

"Why are you smiling at me like that?" I wiped my eyes. "This is not a time for smiles." Suddenly I flung Mark The Pillow across the room.

He landed in a corner, upside down. "And you

can stay there!" I yelled. "Don't think I care!"

I went into the kitchen for a glass of water.

When I came back, Mark The Pillow was still in the corner, looking dejected. I felt sorry for him. I picked him up and brushed him off.

Maybe it wasn't Mark's fault he was with Pamela, who was beautiful and older. Maybe *she* had asked *him* to the movies. Did I expect him to turn her down? How selfish!

"Did I hurt you?" I plumped up Mark The Pillow. His smile thanked me, and I realized why his eyes looked so unconcerned. He had glasses, but no eyelashes. Imagine that. All this time, the poor fellow had been lashless. I got out the felt-tip pen and took care of that.

"Thanks! Much better," Mark The Pillow said in his most manly voice. "Now, can I kiss you again?"

"Oh! I'll have to think about that."

Mark The Pillow continued smiling, although I could tell he felt not only dejected again, but also rejected.

"Did you kiss you-know-who, the girl with white eyebrows?" I asked sternly.

Mark The Pillow didn't change his expression. He just kept smiling.

I searched his face intently. Was that a sly maybe-I-did-kiss-her smile? Or a smug what-do-you-expect smile? Or was it an open, friendly of-course-not, would-I-kiss-another-girl smile?

Or was it none of the above, but, instead, a smile that said, *Sarabeth, you will never know the answer to that question.*

CHAPTER 35

Grant, Patty, Asa, Jennifer, and I were all in the mall one day, just goofing around, when we saw Mark coming toward us.

"Mark The Pillow," Jennifer muttered. We all started laughing insanely.

"Stop," Grant said. "We have to stop." But the closer Mark came, the less we were able to stop.

"Hi, Mark," I got out.

"Hi, Sarabeth." He looked at the others. "Hi, Patty. Grant."

"I'm Asa," Asa said perkily.

"And this is Mark," Jennifer said, "the guy who doesn't know how to pick up a phone or tell a girl anything straight out."

I couldn't believe she'd said it.

Mark's ears and forehead turned pink, then red.

"Remember me, Mark?" Jennifer went on sweetly. She was chewing gum. She made a bubble and popped it in his face. "I'm Jennifer Rosen. We went to Hillside Elementary School together."

Mark didn't say anything. He gave me a quick look that asked, *What's going on?*

"Remember the time you brought that filthy cat into class?" Jennifer said.

We were all standing in front of Mark. He shook his head slowly.

"You don't remember?" Patty said. "Amazing."

"We remember," Grant said. "We remember everything."

"That was a memorable day," Jennifer said. "You sure were a cute little kid back then. But people change, don't they?"

Mark's mouth was open, but nothing came out.

"Well, see you around," Jennifer said.

"Yes! See you around," Grant said.

"See you around," we all said.

"See ya," he mumbled finally and walked away.

"Was that mean of us?" I said. "Were we mean to him?"

"What did we do? We didn't hardly do enough," Jennifer said. "Just said *hi* in a friendly way and mentioned a basic character flaw he has. If you want to talk *mean,* it wasn't half as mean as the way he led you on, Silver!"

"I don't think he meant to lead me on."

"You still like him," Asa said. "Sarabeth! Where's your backbone?"

"I can't help it, Asa. Just seeing him . . . you know what I mean. How about you and Richard?"

"No, no, no, no," Asa said. "That's different. Richard doesn't kiss me one day and show up with another girl the next."

"He better not, anyway, if he knows what's good for him," Grant said.

"Listen, everyone," Jennifer said. "We have to help Silver get over this crush on Mark. I think she should go home and kick Mark The Pillow around."

"I tried, Jen, but I just ended up feeling sorry for him. It's not his fault he likes angel eyebrows."

"Silver, you can't feel sorry for someone who's done you dirt."

"Jen's right," Patty said.

"Really, I'm all right," I said. "I feel that I'm over him."

"Completely over him?"

"Well . . . nearly completely."

"Not good enough," Jen said. She linked arms with me. And then, on some impulse, without asking each other, we all turned at the same moment and started walking fast after Mark.

Poor Mark.

Poor, poor Mark. He didn't know what was in store for him.